J
F
Low

Lowry, Lois

Anastasia at this address

054373

SPEEDWAY PUBLIC LIBRARY
5633 W 25th St
SPEEDWAY IN 46224

ANASTASIA
AT THIS ADDRESS

ANASTASIA
AT THIS ADDRESS

Lois Lowry

Houghton Mifflin Company
Boston   1991

054373

Library of Congress Cataloging-in-Publication Data

Lowry, Lois.
  Anastasia at this address / by Lois Lowry.
    p. cm.
  Summary: Ready for romance, thirteen-year-old Anastasia answers an
ad in the personals with an exaggerated description of herself but
soon runs into trouble when the unknown man turns up at a friend's
wedding.
  ISBN 0-395-56263-5
  [1. Letter writing—Fiction. 2. Humorous stories.] I. Title.
PZ7.L9673Amcm 1991   90-48308
[Fic]—dc20   CIP
                         AC

Printed in the United States of America

AGM 10 9 8 7 6 5 4 3 2 1

ANASTASIA
AT THIS ADDRESS

"Mom, I need you to tell me what a word means." Anastasia peered through the doorway into the studio, where her mother was working on some book illustrations.

Mrs. Krupnik looked up from the table where she'd been leaning over a large sheet of paper covered with an intricate pen-and-ink drawing. "What word?" she asked.

"Gwem," Anastasia said.

"*Gwem?*" Katherine Krupnik put her pen down and stared at Anastasia. "Never heard of it. Is it English?"

Anastasia nodded. "Yeah," she said. "But maybe the vowel is wrong. It could be gwim. Or gwam."

"Guam is an island in the Pacific. Are you doing Geography homework?"

Anastasia made a face. "No. Not Guam. I should have spelled it for you. It's with a *W*. G-w-a-m. Or gwem, or gwim."

Her mother shook her head. "Did you look in the dictionary?"

"It's not there. But I know it's a word because I read it in a magazine."

"Well," said Mrs. Krupnik, "they made a mistake. Or maybe it's a misprint. There's no such word as gwem. Or gwam. Or gwim."

Anastasia frowned. "How about gwum? It could be gwum."

Mrs. Krupnik grinned. "Aha!" she said. "*Gwum*. That one I know."

"What does it mean?"

"Well, a person with a slight speech impediment? If that person is sad or depressed? He's gwum. A wittle bit gwum and gwoomy."

"Ha-ha," Anastasia said sarcastically. "*You're* no help."

"Sorry," her mother said. "Take a look at this, as long as you're here, would you?" She turned the paper in front of her so that Anastasia could see it. "Do the proportions look right to you? It seems to me that the guy's arms are a little too long."

Anastasia walked over to the drawing table and peered at the sketch, a complicated one that showed a pudgy farmer leading a long line of cows through a meadow.

"No," she said, after a moment. "His arms look just

fine to me. I don't know how you do it, Mom. I can't draw *anything,* but you just whip off these fabulous pictures with no trouble at all."

"What do you mean, 'whip off'? I went to art school for four long years, Anastasia, learning how to do this. My parents spent thousands of dollars of tuition so that I could draw cows with silly grins. Look at this one, with the daffodil hanging out of her mouth — isn't she cute?"

Her mother pointed to the cow, and Anastasia nodded.

"But I always have trouble drawing *people,*" her mother said with a sigh. "Darn it. All those *years* of Life class —"

"I gotta go, Mom," Anastasia said quickly. "I'm sorry I interrupted you. His arms are just fine, really."

She fled, closing the door to the studio behind her.

Anastasia hated it when her mother mentioned Life class. Life class was a terrible thing they did in art schools. It was a fake name: "Life." It made you think they would teach you something profound, something about the meaning of life. But they didn't at all. It was *really* a class that taught you to draw people. *Nude* people. And let's face it, Anastasia thought, nude was just another word for, ugh, *naked.*

What if *nuns* decided to go to art school, to learn to make nice religious drawings, of saints and stuff? And the nuns would go off happily to Life class, for Pete's sake, thinking they would learn about the meaning of life — a thing that nuns were certainly interested in — and they would go into that room very innocent and nunlike, and — whammo. Naked people standing around. Anastasia shuddered, just thinking of it. Probably art schools all over the country were filled with unconscious nuns being carted away on stretchers, their faces pale with shock.

"Gross," Anastasia muttered, feeling sorry for nuns. She wandered back into her dad's study and picked up the *New York Review of Books*.

It was a truly boring magazine, Anastasia thought, but it had a couple of interesting pages at the end of each issue. She turned to the page she'd been reading and looked at the word again. Gwem. Or gwam. Or gwim. She wondered why they hadn't put in the vowel. It was *very* frustrating, not knowing what the word meant.

"Hi, sport. Are you turning literary all of a sudden? There's a great article in there on the politics of Elizabethan poetry." Anastasia's father came into the study, set his briefcase on the couch, and reached for one of his pipes from the assortment that stood in a rack on his desk.

"Hi, Dad. Look at this, would you? Do *you* know what this word means?" Anastasia pointed to it. She read aloud: " 'Gwem, slender, thirty-five, loves sunsets, Schubert, Springsteen, and spaghetti.' "

"*Gwem?*" Her father peered over her shoulder with a puzzled look. "Oh. That's not gwem, Dumbo. It's an abbreviation, GWM. It means Gay White Male."

"But what about this one, farther down?" Anastasia

4

read some more: " 'Dijof, petite and pretty, forty-two, seeks soulmate who appreciates Woody Allen, woodstoves, and Wordsworth.' "

"Easy," her father said, lighting his pipe. "DJF. Divorced Jewish Female."

"Oh! Then — let's see — SBM wouldn't be sabim! Stupid me, I thought it was sabim! It would be —"

"Single Black Male."

"Oh, *neat!* It's like a puzzle! Here's a Divorced White Female — DWF — who's looking for a dentist with a sense of humor —"

"Lotsa luck," her father, who had recently had gum surgery, muttered.

"And here's — hey, listen, Dad, this one sounds like you! MWM. That would be Married White Male, right? Just like you?"

"Right. What else does it say?"

" 'Married White Male, forty-eight' — that's just your age, Dad — 'Ivy League background, needs companion occasional New York weekends,' " Anastasia read, " 'theater, long walks, snuggling.' " She looked up. "*Snuggling?* A married guy, *snuggling?*"

Her father shrugged and rolled his eyes.

Anastasia glared at him. "That's not you, is it?" she asked suspiciously. "You're not planning New York weekends, are you?"

Her father groaned. "You know I hate New York," he said. "And I hate long walks. And my weekends are taken. I snuggle with your mother, every weekend. Where *is* she, speaking of your mother? And where's your brother?"

Anastasia closed the *New York Review of Books*. "She's working, in the studio. And Sam's playing at his friend Adam's. They'll be bringing him home soon. Can I keep this?"

"May," her father said. He was looking through the stack of mail on his desk.

"It's not May, it's March," Anastasia pointed out.

"I was correcting your grammar. *May* I keep this. Yes, you may. It's last week's; I'm through with it. Read the article about the politics of Elizabethan poetry. Impress the heck out of your seventh-grade English teacher."

Anastasia scowled. There were enormous disadvantages to having a father who was an English professor, even if he *was* an MWM, 48, Ivy League background.

She tucked the magazine under her arm and headed upstairs to her bedroom, on the third floor. To her bedroom, where her desk was. To her desk, where her best fineline Rollerball pen was. She planned to write a letter.

Anastasia was going to write to SWM, 28, boyish charm, inherited wealth, looking for tall young woman, nonsmoker, to share Caribbean vacations, reruns of *Casablanca*, and romance.

Anastasia was only thirteen. But fifteen years didn't seem too much of an age difference. Anastasia's father was ten years older than her mother, for Pete's sake. The important thing was being on the same wavelength. Her parents were definitely on the same wavelength.

6

And Anastasia was quite certain that she was on the same wavelength as SWM. She was 5'7", which was tall. She was young. She hated smoking. She had watched the old movie *Casablanca* so many times that she could recite some of the dialogue by heart. She thought she would like Caribbean vacations, though she had never experienced one.

And she was *definitely* ready for romance.

Dear SWM,

I apologize for not using the proper heading on this letter. I am a well-educated SWF and my education just last year included the writing of a Friendly Letter, and I know I should put the date and my address and all of that. And my name, at the end, after "Yours truly."

And this *is* a Friendly Letter. But it seems like an unusual situation. Rick in *Casablanca* would understand that, and I'm quite sure *he* wouldn't put the proper heading on a Friendly Letter. He would use a code name, too, the way you have. And I will, too.

You should use my code name on the envelope when you reply, because — as Rick knew, in *Casablanca* — there are spies everywhere.

I am a tall young woman who has never smoked, not *once*, even when I have been with friends who tried to tempt me into trying it.

I don't spend *all* my time watching *Casablanca*. Sometimes, when I am not watching *Casablanca*, I am reading the *New York Review of Books*, especially parts like "The Politics of Elizabethan Poetry." I always find it amazing that there are so many poets named Elizabeth, don't you?

Unfortunately I have not inherited wealth, as you have. But I have inherited my grandmother's wedding ring, which I keep in my little carved wooden box that also holds other treasures. When you reply to this letter I will put your reply in my carved wooden box.

Do you have any hobbies besides watching *Casablanca*?

Yours truly,
SWIFTY

(Single White Intelligent Female: Tall Young)

2

Tall, Eclectic. Ivy
seeks erudite, music
sharing, caring, and fun.

SWM, 28. Boyish charm, r
inherited wealth, looking
non-smoker, to share Car
re-runs of Casablanca, and

"I've decided to give up men," Anastasia's friend Sonya Isaacson announced suddenly.

It was a startling statement. But Anastasia barely heard it, and she paid no attention. She was walking home from school with her three best friends, and she was thinking about SWM. She was wondering if his letter might be there today, on the hall table, when she got home. A week had passed since Anastasia had carefully stamped the envelope she had addressed to the New York box number and, after holding her breath to the count of ten, for good luck, slipped the letter into the mailbox on the corner near her house.

She had already thought through the obvious pitfalls connected to his response. What if SWM knew someone who lived in her town? What if he inquired casually of the friend, "Do you know someone named Anastasia Krupnik?" And what if the friend *did?*

And what if the friend *laughed* and said, "That skinny seventh-grader? The one with the big glasses?"

Well, *that* could doom a potentially fulfilling relationship.

But she had cleverly prevented that possibility by using the code name.

And she had foreseen, also, the problem of her parents. She had visualized her mother, who usually picked up the day's mail from the hall floor after the mailman pushed it through the slot, puzzling over the frequent letters from New York. Her mother — who was much too inquisitive, no question — would surely say, "Anastasia, who is this person writing to you from New York every other day? Why does this person call you 'Swifty'? And what is this S.W.A.K. this person puts on the back of the envelopes?" (Anastasia was quite certain that it wouldn't be very long before the correspondence reached the every-other-day, S.W.A.K. stage.)

So she had slyly prepared her parents.

"Funniest thing," she said casually at dinner one evening. "I have a nickname, at school. *Everyone* calls me by my nickname."

"Oh?" her mother replied. "What is it?"

"Ah, Swifty," Anastasia said. "Cute, huh?"

"*Swifty?*" her parents said in unison.

"Yeah. Swifty. I guess because I'm so swift at stuff.

I'm very swift at, ah, diagramming sentences in English. Everybody notices how swift I am. And now they've just started calling me Swifty. May I have some more salad, please?"

Deftly she changed the subject. But she had planted the beginning of the necessary information.

The next night, she planted the rest.

"Did you guys ever have pen pals when you were kids?" she asked.

"Nope," her father said. "I hated writing letters when I was a kid. I still do."

"*I* had a pen pal," Mrs. Krupnik said. "Someone who lived in France. Her name was Yvonne. We wrote to each other for about a year, when I was in ninth grade. I wonder what ever happened to her."

"Can I have a pen pal?" Sam asked.

"Sure. When you're older," his mother replied.

"Why not now?" asked Sam, pouting.

"Because I can't trust you with a pen," Mrs. Krupnik said. "You write on things you're not supposed to."

Sam nodded. "Like your bedspread," he muttered.

"Right. Like my bedspread," Mrs. Krupnik said angrily.

They had *almost* veered away from the topic, but Anastasia interrupted.

"You might notice that I'll be getting letters soon," she said.

"Oh? From a pen pal?" her mother asked.

"Yes," Anastasia said. "May I have some more

salad, please?"

"Sure. Pass your plate. You're becoming a real salad-lover, Anastasia."

"You may call me by my nickname if you like," Anastasia said. "You do remember my nickname, don't you?"

Her mother nodded and handed the plate back. "I think I'll stick with your given name, if you don't mind," she said. "I'm not real crazy about Swifty."

"Well," said Anastasia, poking the lettuce on her plate with her fork, "I only mentioned it because you might notice that my pen pal calls me that."

"I'm going to have a nickname, too," Sam announced. "Macho-man. That's my nickname."

Anastasia smiled slightly. She had done it. She had implanted all the necessary information without creating a big deal.

Maybe, in her future life, she could be a successful spy.

*

"I'm giving men up completely. Cold turkey," Sonya went on.

Anastasia blinked. She hadn't been paying any attention. But Daphne and Meredith had both stopped walking and turned to stare at Sonya, who had a determined look on her chubby freckled face. Anastasia stared at her, too.

"Sonya," she pointed out, "that's like giving up smoking when you've never even smoked. It doesn't *mean* anything."

"Right," Daphne Bellingham agreed, nodding her blond head in its bright blue knitted hat. "How can you give up men when you were never involved with them to begin with?"

Sonya frowned. "Well," she said, "I phrased it wrong. I meant that I've decided to give up the *pursuit* of men."

All four girls shifted their schoolbooks in their arms and began walking again.

"Why?" Anastasia asked after a moment. Secretly, she was remembering the letter she had mailed last week. She felt as if she had just *begun* a pursuit. And now one of her best friends was renouncing the same pursuit.

"It takes up too much time," Sonya explained. "I seem to spend all my time trying to figure out ways — *schemes*, actually — to get Norman Berkowitz to like me. I could be spending that time doing worthwhile things."

"Like what?" Meredith Halberg asked. "What could be more worthwhile than chasing boys?"

Sonya shrugged. "I could be working on a cure for cancer. Or knitting mittens for homeless people. Or — I don't know. *Anything.* Just about anything would be more worthwhile than chasing Norman Berkowitz all the time."

"Are you really *truly* going to give it up?" Anastasia asked. She was impressed. Sonya had been pursuing Norman Berkowitz for months now, throughout their seventh-grade year. It was a part of her life, the way

13

pursuing Eddie Cox was part of Daphne's and pursuing Kirby McEvedy was part of Meredith's and — well, yes, she'd admit it — pursuing Steve Harvey had been part of Anastasia's life until she'd discovered this new man whose interests seemed to be more like her own.

She hadn't told her friends about the new man in her life.

"I don't know what I'd do with myself if I gave up the pursuit of Kirby McEvedy," Meredith said, wrinkling her forehead. "It's what I think about, starting when I get up every morning. My mom accuses me of thinking about nothing but clothes, but she doesn't realize it's really Kirby McEvedy."

"I have all these lists in my room," Daphne said, "of every place I've ever seen Eddie Cox, and when. McDonald's on Thursday afternoon, for example. The public library once, on a Saturday. Waiting for a bus on the corner of Central Street — that was also a Saturday, at 10:17 A.M.."

"Do you follow him around?" Anastasia asked in amazement.

"Sort of. Just to keep track of where he goes and what he does so that I can start appearing at the same places as if by accident," Daphne admitted.

"Doesn't that take a lot of your time, sleuthing around like that?"

Daphne sighed. "Every waking minute. I miss a lot of good stuff on TV. And it's why I didn't have time to finish *Johnny Tremain* for English class. I couldn't

14

explain that to Mr. Rafferty, of course, so I had to tell him that I lost the book."

"*See?*" Sonya said loudly. "Every one of us, we're sacrificing our lives for this stupid pursuit of men. Meredith, if you didn't spend all your time thinking about Kirby, you could think about clothes instead, or something else equally worthwhile. And Daphne — you could have gotten an A on the *Johnny Tremain* test if you hadn't been spying on Eddie Cox instead. And Anastasia —"

"Forget it," Anastasia interrupted her. "I already figured it out for myself, Sonya. And I hadn't told you guys yet, but I've already given up the pursuit of Steve Har——? Harcourt? Hartley? See? I can't even remember his last name."

Her friends began to laugh. They had reached Sonya's house and stopped at the end of the long driveway.

"I'll see you guys in the morning," Sonya said. She looked at her watch. "Four o'clock. Great. I have time to do my homework, start reading a book for extra credit, wash my hair, make some brownies, iron my gymsuit. Maybe I'll paint my bedroom. In the old days, of course, I would just be holed up in my room, plotting and scheming, writing Norman Berkowitz's name all over my notebook. What a relief to be finished with such adolescent pursuits."

Anastasia, Meredith, and Daphne watched Sonya walk up the driveway toward her house.

"Look," Anastasia pointed out. "She has a new, mature look to her. A more self-confident walk. A self-assured way of holding her shoulders."

"What a woman," Daphne murmured in an awed voice. "I admire her."

"I'm going to do it, too," Meredith announced. "This is it, guys. I've given up men." She took a deep breath. "I'm trembling. It was tough. But I think I'm going to make it."

"Good for you, Mer," Anastasia said. "It *is* tough. I know, because I already gave up Steve What's-his-name."

"That leaves only me," Daphne said. "And I suppose I should join you. You know, my *mother's* given up men. Ever since she and my dad got divorced and she became a feminist. She quit curling her hair and everything. She doesn't even wear lipstick anymore. She says makeup is just a stupid ploy to attract men. She threw all her Revlon products away."

"I admire that," Anastasia said fervently.

"What about deodorant?" Meredith asked uncertainly. "Can you still use deodorant if you give up men?"

Daphne nodded. "Yeah. My mom does. Deodorant's okay. But no perfume."

They began to walk toward the apartment building where Daphne lived with her mother. Each afternoon, after school, the four girls took a circuitous route so that they could see each other home. Today was the day that Sonya Isaacson's house was first and Anastasia's was last.

Sometimes they arranged their route so that they would pass the houses of Eddie Cox, Steve Harvey, Kirby McEvedy, and Norman Berkowitz. On the days when they casually walked past all the boys' houses, they didn't reach their own homes until almost dark.

"Look at that," Daphne said, standing on the steps to her building. "See the clock on the front of the bank over there? Four-twenty. Look at the *time* we save if we don't prowl around looking for men! That does it. I'm joining up. No more pursuit of Eddie Cox."

"Your mom will be proud of you," Anastasia told her. "But, Daph — and Meredith — could we call them *boys?* I mean, instead of *men?*"

They pondered that.

"No more pursuit of boys," Daphne said. "Yeah, okay. I never pursued men, anyway."

"Okay," Meredith agreed. "We've given up boys. We can do our homework for a change."

"And watch *Wheel of Fortune,*" Daphne pointed out, grinning. She waved and went inside her building.

Anastasia and Meredith trudged on, talking about how their grades would improve, how they'd be more helpful around the house, how proud Mother Teresa would be if she only knew, how they could get involved in community projects now that every waking moment wouldn't be consumed by thoughts of boys.

At the Halbergs' house, Meredith's older sister, Kirsten, was just pulling away from the curb in her

17

ancient red Volkswagen. She waved at the girls and beeped her horn in greeting.

Meredith shook her head in disgust, looking after the departing car. "She's probably going to go pick up Jeff at work and then they'll go out to dinner and discuss wedding plans. That's all they do, she and Jeff. Wedding plans, wedding plans. *Sick.*"

"I remember that your sister was once a fine young woman," Anastasia said sadly. "Intelligent and ambitious."

"A waste of a young life," Meredith acknowledged mournfully.

Anastasia said goodbye and walked the remaining two blocks to her own house alone. She realized that she felt a little guilty. No, actually, she felt more than a little; she felt *massively* guilty. It was true that she had given up her pursuit of Steve Harvey. It was true that she, like her friends, would become a better person: more scholarly, more family-oriented, better read, more civic-minded and politically aware, now that she would not be wasting her time trying to get an idiotic seventh-grade boy to pay attention to her.

But *men?* That was something else again. She had not given up on SWM.

Anastasia had been calculating very carefully: the number of days it might take for her letter to reach New York; the number of minutes, maybe even an hour or two, for SWM to compose his reply; the number of days for his reply to make its way from Manhattan to the Krupnik mail slot in a Boston suburb.

It might — just *might* — be today.

She hurried up the steps to her house, opened the front door, and called, "Hello! I'm home!" at the same time that she was scattering the stacked mail on the hall table, looking for a letter addressed to Swifty.

But it was not there. Not yet.

Dear SWM,

I know that it is just the tiniest bit rude to write a second time when I have not yet received your answer to my first letter.

But I saw on the TV news (I am very interested in current events and things of international interest, like for example rumors of marital trouble between Charles and Diana) that a postal vehicle in New York collided with a truck carrying live chickens. Peter Jennings on the news made it sound like a funny event, and they showed pictures of live chickens running around the street, with people chasing them.

But I didn't find it at all amusing. For one thing, the chickens looked very scared and the people chasing them didn't look too thrilled either.

And also: Peter Jennings didn't even mention the possibility of mail getting lost as a result of that accident.

I thought I had better write again just in case my first letter was on that truck and got mixed in with all those chicken feathers and was lost.

Or maybe you are sick. The news also said that there's a lot of flu around. I really am concerned for you.

I want to tell you, also, that I did have a relationship in my life. I concealed it from you before. But now it is completely over, so it need not come between us in any way. His name was Steve. He was also a SWM.

Take aspirin and drink lots of liquids, if you have flu. It is okay to write letters even if you have a slight fever. My brother had a slight fever when he had chicken pox but he was able to do a lot of coloring and follow-the-dots with no problem.

Sincerely,
SWIFTY

(Single Waiting Impatient Female: Tall, Young)

3

It was a usual sort of Thursday evening dinner at the Krupniks' house. Anastasia's parents were arguing, in a friendly fashion, about a novel they had both been reading. Myron Krupnik was really an expert on books, since he was a professor of literature, so he made a long almost-speech, as if he were standing in front of his Harvard classroom, and he helped himself to more pot roast at the same time.

"The futuristic setting's effective, I'll grant you," he said, carefully lifting a slice of meat from the serving plate to his own, "but it's too distracting. It's self-indulgent. The entire theme would have been enhanced if she — whoops. Sorry." He began to dab with his napkin at the splotch of gravy he had dripped on the tablecloth.

"That's okay. Leave it," Anastasia's mother said. "Sam, do you want some more meat while Daddy's slicing it?"

Anastasia's brother looked up from his plate, where he had carefully arranged four pieces of carrot in a line, like the cars of a train. "One square piece, for a caboose," he said. "Please," he added politely.

Dr. Krupnik used the point of the carving knife to create a small square of pot roast. He lifted it to Sam's plate and placed it neatly at the end of the train. "You know," he said thoughtfully, looking at the arrangement on Sam's plate, "if we took a good-size potato and dug through it with a spoon, we could make a heck of a tunnel for that train."

"*Myron,*" Mrs. Krupnik said in a meaningful voice.

"Sorry," he replied. "I lost my head. Sam, old sport, eat your train so that you can have some dessert."

"I will," Sam told him. "In a minute." He had taken a large potato from the serving bowl and was about to dig a tunnel through it.

Anastasia, watching her family as she ate her own dinner, was thinking. Mainly she was thinking about marriage. If it was true, what she and her friends had agreed on this afternoon, that the pursuit of boys took up valuable time which could be better spent on more worthwhile activities, then what about *marriage*, for Pete's sake? Marriage was even *more* time-consuming.

Look at her father at this very moment, for example. He had degrees from several famous universities, and he taught at a very famous university, and he had published several pretty famous books of poetry. But at this very moment, when he had begun to make a profound statement about literature, his attention had been diverted. And now — Anastasia glanced over again, and it was true — now her father, forty-eight years old and balding and bearded, was hunched over, helping a three-year-old dig a tunnel through a potato as if it were the most important enterprise in the world.

Marriage had done that to him.

And look at her mother, too, Anastasia thought. Look at Katherine Krupnik, graduate of art school, award-winning illustrator of children's books. Had she, today, worked industriously on a painting that would catapult her to fame in the art world? Had Katherine Krupnik *created* anything today? Anastasia asked herself the question and answered it, sadly, for herself as well. She felt a huge twinge of pity for her talented mother.

The only thing Katherine Krupnik had created today was a pot roast. A pretty *good* pot roast, to be sure; but nonetheless, a pot roast.

Marriage had thwarted her mother's life.

"I have decided that I'm against marriage," Anastasia announced to her family.

"That's *another* thing," her father said, looking up from the potato. But he wasn't talking to Anastasia; he was talking to her mother. Anastasia realized he was referring to the book they'd been discussing. "Granted, she's making her point through satire. But she's taken the basic institution and completely perverted it through a warped, feminist eye."

"You're an absolute idiot, Myron," Anastasia's mother said, "if you see that novel as feminist."

"I see myself as a feminist," Anastasia said loudly. "I'm giving up makeup and other stuff that is just designed to attract boys."

Sam burst into tears suddenly. "It fell in!" he bellowed. "My dumb tunnel just fell in!" He stabbed the broken potato angrily with his fork.

"And perfume, too," Anastasia said over Sam's wails. "Not deodorant, but perfume. I've renounced it, along with marriage."

"Well," her mother said tensely, "I do hope you haven't renounced dishwashing. Because tonight's your turn. Yours and your dad's.

"Sam," she said firmly, "you are off to bed this instant, without dessert. Your table manners are deplorable.

"And I," Mrs. Krupnik added, "am going to take a long bath and I'm going to finish reading this brilliant novel that some morons can't appreciate." She glared meaningfully at her husband, then picked up Sam, who was still howling, and headed toward the hallway and the stairs.

"See what I mean about marriage?" Anastasia asked her father as they cleared the table.

He grinned and ate the remains of Sam's train.

*

The telephone rang just as Anastasia handed the last washed plate to her father, who was wearing a plaid apron, holding a soggy striped dishtowel, and smoking his pipe.

"Hello?" Anastasia tucked the receiver against her shoulder and held it there with her head while she dried her hands.

"It's for me," she told her father. "It's Meredith Halberg."

She listened to her friend's voice for a minute.

"She *what?*" Anastasia said in gleeful amazement. *"Really?* She's not just kidding?"

She tilted her head toward her father, who was putting the final plate into the cupboard. "Guess what! Meredith's sister, Kirsten? She wants — wait a minute, Dad — I have to get more details.

"Meredith? When is it? Where is it? And how does it work? I mean, tell me absolutely everything!"

Dr. Krupnik hung his dishtowel on the rack to dry. He wiped the kitchen counter with a sponge, turned off the light over the sink, took a pear from the bowl of fruit on the table, and left the kitchen, still smoking his pipe and tossing the pear back and forth between his hands.

Two seconds later, Anastasia sped past him in the hall as he headed toward his study to watch the evening news on TV.

"Excuse me, Dad. I have to find Mom and tell her the most exciting news I've maybe ever had in my whole life!

"You can go watch Peter Jennings talk about world events if you want to, Dad," she continued as she bounded up the stairs, "but in all honesty, the most interesting news in the whole world is happening right here, right in the suburbs of Boston, Massachusetts, and it's happening right to your very own daughter. So if I were you, Dad, I'd forget Peter Jennings for just one night and come upstairs and listen to what I'm about to tell Mom!

"Mom!" Anastasia called from the stairs. "Guess *what!*"

Myron Krupnik, still holding a pear and with his pipe clenched between his teeth, stood in the doorway of the study. He eyed the television set. He *never* missed Peter Jennings and the evening news. He wanted very much to know what had happened today in China, and in Kuwait, and in Rumania. His *Boston Globe* was in the study, too, folded on his desk where he had dropped it when he got home from work; and he very much wanted to read the *Globe* and see if the Celtics had won the night before and what the weather would be; and he wanted to read "Doonesbury," and . . .

Myron Krupnik took a last look at his study, sighed, and headed up the stairs after his daughter.

"Mom, sit down so you don't faint when I tell you this," Anastasia was saying dramatically.

Katherine Krupnik stared at her. "Anastasia, I'm in *bed.* I'm already *lying* down."

That was true. Mrs. Krupnik had taken a bath after

dinner and she was in bed, leaning against a pile of pillows with her book propped on her knees. She was wearing the oversize Harvard T-shirt that she usually wore instead of a nightgown.

Anastasia sat down on the end of her parents' bed. Her father leaned against the doorframe and puffed on his pipe.

"Meredith called," Anastasia explained. "You know her sister Kirsten is about to get married? Her parents used to be really upset about that because Kirsten hasn't finished college yet, but they've finally adjusted to it because Jeff — Kirsten's fiancé — is a really nice guy, and he has a good job and everything, and Kirsten promised she'll go back and do her senior year, and she won't have babies right away, and —"

Myron Krupnik looked at his watch. It was just about time for Peter Jennings's first commercial break. "Could you get to the point a little more quickly, Anastasia?" he suggested politely.

Katherine Krupnik's eyes flickered down to the paragraph she'd been reading. She turned a page of her novel. "Mmmm," she said. "I know all of that already, Anastasia."

"Well, here's the thing," Anastasia went on. "She's being married at the Congregational church at the beginning of May, and she's *hoping* that the lilacs will be in bloom, because she *really* wants the church decorated with white lilacs, but if they're not blooming that week, it'll cost a *fortune* to get lilacs from some other place, and her parents aren't sure they'll be willing to do that. So she might have to settle for some other kind of flowers —"

Dr. Krupnik glanced at his watch. Mrs. Krupnik glanced at her book.

"— and the reception's at the country club. Dinner, for two hundred people. *Probably* chicken. They had a couple of choices, but filet mignon is just out of the question, Mr. Halberg said, because it costs so much, and anyway, people don't expect filet mignon at a wedding reception. Heck, they don't really care what they eat, so chicken's all right, don't you think? I do."

"Anastasia," her mother said in an exasperated voice, "*please* get to the point."

"Well," Anastasia squealed, "the point is: Jeff has two sisters who were going to be the bridesmaids, and now *both* of them are pregnant and their bridesmaid's dresses don't fit anymore, so they had to back out, and Kirsten had an absolute tantrum, Meredith said. She was so upset, because the wedding's only six weeks away, and then her mom had a great idea, and guess what it is!"

"What?" her mother asked.

"She wants me to be a junior bridesmaid!"

"A what?" her mother asked.

"A junior bridesmaid! Me and Meredith and Sonya and Daphne! All four of us! And it's just the same as bridesmaid. Really, Mom, you get to wear a long dress and carry flowers and be in the official photographs, and your name is in the paper. And it's not babyish like being a flower girl, Mom, don't think that for one minute!"

"Excuse me," Myron Krupnik murmured. "I want to catch the last of the news." He went downstairs, leaving a little cloud of pipe smoke behind in the doorway.

"Anastasia," her mother said, "just tonight, at dinner, barely an hour ago, you said that you had renounced marriage. I remember your saying that."

Anastasia sighed. Sometimes her mother missed the point of things completely.

"*Marriage*, Mom," she explained patiently. "I renounced marriage. Not *weddings!*"

Dear SWM,

I know you have not gotten my last letter yet, and are probably not even over the flu, if you have it.

But I felt that it was important for you to know that I have renounced makeup and perfume and marriage.

I have not renounced romance or Humphrey Bogart movies or cruises in the Caribbean.

How do you feel about the question of filet mignon versus chicken? You're not a vegetarian or anything, are you? I wouldn't *mind* if you are a vegetarian because I am a very accepting person but I feel I must tell you that I really like pepperoni on my pizza. I know a place where you can get them half pepperoni and half mushroom, though, so we could get along pretty well even if you are a vegetarian. Like Jack Spratt and his wife, ha-ha.

I do hope you are well enough by now to get out to the mailbox. Bundle up real good.

Sincerely,
SWIFTY

(Solitary Wistful Impatient Female: Tall, Young)

4

"Do we get to wear high heels?" Daphne asked.

Anastasia groaned. "I hope not," she said. "I'm *already* taller than everybody in the whole world except Larry Bird."

Kirsten Halberg steered her little VW carefully into a small parking place in the crowded lot at the shopping mall. "Here we are," she said. "Lock the door on your side. I don't want my car stolen a month before my wedding."

Anastasia, Daphne, Meredith, and Sonya climbed out of the tiny car and stretched their legs. They locked the door on the passenger side and closed it tightly.

Kirsten turned and surveyed the four of them.

"Now," she said, "let's get this straight. It's *my* wedding. So I get the final decision on stuff. Right?"

"Right." The girls all nodded.

"No high heels. Flats, okay? I don't want you guys tripping and stumbling down the aisle. That's decision one. Agreed?"

Anastasia nodded enthusiastically. Daphne, Meredith, and Sonya, who all wanted to wear high heels, made faces. But they nodded, too.

"And as for color —" Kirsten went on.

"Oh, *please* not pink," begged Sonya. "Not with my red hair. Anything but pink, *please*, Kirsten."

"Okay, not pink," Kirsten agreed.

"Please not green?" Daphne said. "Green makes me look weird."

Kirsten sighed. "Listen," she said, "I had blue in mind. Does anybody have any violent negative feelings about blue?"

Everyone was silent. Anastasia thought about blue. She thought about herself in a long blue dress. Walking down an aisle. With everyone looking, in awe and admiration.

Daphne interrupted her thoughts. "Can it be strapless?" Daphne asked.

Anastasia's fantasy changed. She had been envisioning herself wearing a long blue dress with tiny buttons up to a high lace collar. Now she tried to switch, in her mind, to strapless. But it didn't work. Strapless fell down. She had never been able to figure out what held strapless dresses up, anyway.

She pictured the four of them walking down the aisle, one by one, wearing blue strapless dresses. She pictured their new shoes tripping on the hems of the dresses. She pictured the tops of the dresses falling down. Right in church. One after the other.

She pictured the entire congregation falling out of their pews, doubled up, laughing.

She pictured photographers selling the photographs to *People* magazine.

"BOSTON WEDDING'S A COMPLETE BUST," the caption might say.

"Please not strapless," Anastasia said desperately. "*Please* not strapless. Because what if —"

A nearby car horn beeped. The girls were standing in an empty parking space that the driver of a black Ford Escort wanted to get into. He leaned from his window and called, "I don't care if it's strapless or topless or backless, just move it someplace else so I can park my car!"

"Come on," Kirsten said, and she led the way toward the store where they would choose their junior bridesmaid's dresses.

*

Two hours later all five of them crowded together in a booth at Friendly's, sipping milkshakes. In the empty booth behind them were stacked four large dress boxes and four matching shoeboxes.

"Okay," Kirsten said, "are we friends again?"

One by one they nodded glumly. It had not been an easy shopping expedition.

Kirsten turned to Daphne. "You understand why I

said no to the slinky black velvet?"

Daphne was still sulking a little. "Yeah," she admitted reluctantly. "It really would've looked cool on me. But maybe not at a wedding. I see your point."

"Sonya?" Kirsten turned to Sonya, who was sucking disconsolately on her straw. "Your feelings aren't still hurt, are they? The saleslady was a jerk. You shouldn't take it personally."

Sonya set aside her half-finished milkshake. She was still glowering. "Well, she could have said *'plump.'* I don't mind *'plump.'* But I *hate* 'chubby.' Why did she have to say 'chubby'?" She sighed. "No," she said finally, "my feelings aren't still hurt. But I hope she gets run over on her way home from work."

"Meredith?" Kirsten spoke to her sister next. "Are you going to quit complaining?"

Meredith nodded. "Yeah," she said. "But I still don't see why you get to choose everything. It's *always* like that. At home you got to choose the wallpaper for the bathroom, and you got to choose the Christmas tree last year — I really wanted that one with long needles, but you picked out that wimpy-looking one because you felt sorry for it, remember? And —"

"Meredith," the other girls all said, laughing, "it's her wedding, remember?"

"And a few weeks from now," her sister pointed out, "I'll be gone, and you'll be like an only child. You'll get to choose all the wallpapers and Christmas trees from now on."

Meredith began to smile a little. "Yeah, I know,"

she acknowledged.

"Anastasia," Kirsten said, turning toward her in the booth, "you're the only one who hasn't been complaining or arguing or whining. Tell the truth, now. How do you feel about the dresses?"

Slowly Anastasia licked the milkshake mustache from her upper lip. She grinned.

"I adore them," she said fervently.

*

At home that evening, alone in her room, Anastasia tried on the pale blue flower-sprigged dress and the matching blue shoes.

She looked at herself in the wall mirror. The low round neck of the dress curved over her shoulders, and when she held back her thick hair she could see that the line of her neck was slender and graceful.

"What do you think, Frank?" Anastasia asked her goldfish. "Do you think I'll ever be beautiful? Do you think that maybe, with this dress, I'm *starting* to be beautiful?"

Frank Goldfish twirled in his bowl. A few bubbles moved slowly to the surface.

"I know, Frank, your standards are probably a little different," Anastasia said, watching him. "You'd probably prefer wet-look orange, wouldn't you?"

Peering intently into the bowl, Anastasia thought she could see Frank's lips form the word "Yup."

What do *fish* know, Anastasia thought. She turned away from the goldfish bowl, opened the door of her room, and headed downstairs to show her parents.

"Ready for the grand entrance?" she called as she

neared the bottom of the stairs. Her mother and father were in the study watching *This Old House* on TV. Sam was playing on the floor with his Legos.

"I forgot to tell you when you got home, Anastasia," her mother called back. "You got a . . ."

Her voice trailed away as Anastasia entered the study with a dramatic swirl of her long skirt.

"*Wow,*" her mother said.

Sam looked up with wide eyes and popped his thumb into his mouth.

"Shaza——" her father began, but then he remembered that Anastasia absolutely hated it when he said "Shazam."

"Sorry," Dr. Krupnik said. He searched for a different word. He was a university professor of literature and a published author, after all, so he was an expert on language and could always find just the right, the most appropriate, the absolutely most sophisticated word for any occasion.

"*Stupendo!*" he said at last.

Anastasia turned slowly so that they could admire the back of the dress with its bouffant sash. She lifted the hem so that they could admire her low-heeled pale blue shoes, each with its single pearl-buttoned strap.

"What did you forget to tell me, Mom?" she asked, smoothing her skirt.

"Oh." Anastasia's mother reached over to her husband's desk, picked up an envelope, and handed it to Anastasia. "Here you go, Swifty. You got a letter from your pen pal."

36

DEAR FRIEND:

I AM VERY SORRY TO RESPOND TO YOUR LETTER WITH THIS COMPUTER-WRITTEN FORM LETTER THAT LOOKS LIKE SOMETHING FROM PUBLISHERS CLEARING HOUSE.

I ENJOYED READING ALL OF YOUR LETTERS, EVEN THOSE OF THE PERSON WHO HAS SO FAR WRITTEN TO ME THREE TIMES.

BUT THE PROBLEM IS THAT I HAVE RECEIVED, SO FAR, 416 LETTERS AS A RESULT OF THE AD I PUT IN THE *NEW YORK REVIEW OF BOOKS*.

I CAN'T ANSWER THEM ALL INDIVIDUALLY SO I HAVE TO NARROW IT DOWN IN SOME WAY.

I HAVE TO ASK YOU EACH TO SEND ME A PHOTOGRAPH, IF YOU WOULDN'T MIND.

IF IT WOULD BE HELPFUL TO YOU, I WILL MENTION THAT I AM *NOT* INTERESTED IN PURSUING A RELATIONSHIP WITH THE WOMAN WHO RAISES SIAMESE CATS — I AM ALLERGIC TO CATS.

AND TO THE WOMAN WHO LIVES IN SITKA, ALASKA — YOU SOUND LIKE A REALLY TERRIFIC LADY, BUT FRANKLY THE DISTANCE IS TOO GREAT FOR ME.

I AM *VERY* INTERESTED IN THE PERSON WHO HAS HER OWN SLOOP.

BUT PLEASE SEND A PHOTOGRAPH. THEN WE CAN NARROW THINGS DOWN.

SINCERELY,
SEPTIMUS SMITH

5

Dear *friend*. Alone in her bedroom, Anastasia made a face when she read the beginning of the letter a second time. "Friend" was awfully impersonal. "Dear" made it a little better, of course, but *still*: "friend"? Come on.

416 wasn't *that* many. He could have written everyone's name in personally, she thought, even if he had to take a day off from work to do it.

She felt a little annoyed at — Anastasia looked at the signature again, to see SWM's name. She had thought of him as SWM for so long now that a different name felt oddly unfamiliar.

Especially a name like Septimus Smith.

Nothing wrong with Smith. But *Septimus?* What

the heck kind of name was that?

Was he named after a month? Did he have brothers named Octimus and Novimus? Anastasia giggled.

Well, she decided, she would just have to get used to it.

Anastasia Krupnik-Smith, she said to herself.

Not too shabby.

Maybe, if she never got used to Septimus, she could call him by a nickname. Smitty was a nickname, sometimes, for Smith. Maybe she would call him Smitty, or something.

"Good evening," she said in a sophisticated voice to her goldfish, "I'm Anastasia Krupnik-Smith, and this is my husband, Smitty."

Frank Goldfish stared at her with a nonplussed look.

Whoops. For a minute there, she realized with an embarrassed giggle, she'd been thinking about marriage, something she had renounced.

Rereading the letter, Anastasia realized that he had singled her out, even if he had begun the letter badly, with "Dear friend." She decided to forgive him for "Dear friend" because farther along he had actually mentioned her specifically. Out of the 416 people who had sent letters, only one had sent *three* letters.

Obviously Septimus Smith was already just a little bit fascinated with Swifty.

She read on. Siamese cats. No prob. Anastasia hadn't had a cat for years, not since she was about six years old. Her father — just like Septimus Smith —

was allergic to cats.

Sitka, Alaska? Too bad, lady, thought Anastasia. You're out of the running. Back to your dogsled and igloo — Septimus Smith isn't interested.

His address was New York City. Boston was only an hour away by plane. Heck, they could have what magazines like *Cosmopolitan* called a commuter marriage —

Whoops. She'd done it again. Forgotten that she had renounced marriage. Anastasia laughed self-consciously.

She read on.

He was very interested in the lady who had her own sloop. What the heck was a sloop?

Here was where the problem came. Although Septimus Smith had singled her out — "the person who has so far written to me three times" — he clearly was *very* interested in "the person who has her own sloop." He had come right out and said so.

Anastasia didn't know if she had her own sloop or not because she didn't know what a sloop was.

She looked around her room, thinking about the kind of stuff she had. She had neat wallpaper, with people riding old-fashioned bicycles. She had a terrific chair, which had once been in the study until its stuffing began coming out. Her parents had given it to her for her room, and she had covered the torn places in the upholstery by spreading a bright yellow beach towel over the chair.

She had fourteen interesting sweatshirts, which her

mother said was a disgusting number of sweatshirts when one considered the people in Ethiopia, who had no sweatshirts at all.

She had a pretty good bike, down in the garage.

She had hundreds of books; a gift certificate from Benetton, saved ever since her birthday; a fantastic-looking goldfish; a pair of 14-karat gold earrings that had belonged to Aunt Rose (Uncle George had given them to Anastasia after Aunt Rose died, and Anastasia had not had the nerve to ask whether Aunt Rose had been wearing them *when* she died, but maybe it didn't matter); and she had boots from L. L. Bean.

She had programs from several Red Sox games, and one of them had Marty Barrett's autograph on it.

Anastasia realized, looking around, that she had a whole lot of valuable stuff.

But she had a feeling that she probably didn't have a sloop.

Also, she had a funny feeling about Septimus Smith's request for a photograph.

She sighed and wondered how to answer his letter.

BRRRRINNG!

The shrill sound of a bell startled her and made her jump.

Sam poked his head around Anastasia's door. He was smiling mischievously.

BRRRINNNG!

"Cut it out, Sam," Anastasia said. "Quit ringing that. I'm thinking. I have a very important letter to write."

Sam grinned and rang the bell he was holding a third time.

"CUT IT OUT, SAM!"

Anastasia started toward her brother and he scurried away. She followed him down the stairs. He continued ringing the little metal bell, looking back over his shoulder to make certain that Anastasia was still chasing him and still angry. There was nothing Sam liked better than to be chased by his sister.

On the first floor, he ducked into Mrs. Krupnik's studio, where she was working. Anastasia followed him.

"Mom, would you *please* make him stop that?" Anastasia asked angrily, glaring at her brother.

Mrs. Krupnik looked up from her drawing table, where she was working on some pen-and-ink sketches of the pudgy little farmer milking a cow who was wearing wedgies on all four hooves. "Stop what?" she asked. She peered down at Sam. "Sam, what is that in your hand?"

Sam held it up gleefully and pushed hard at the metal switch with his thumb.

BRRRINNNG!

Anastasia and her mother both winced.

"It's the bell off the handle of his tricycle," Anastasia explained, although her mother had recognized the sound. "He took Dad's screwdriver and managed to get it off the bike."

"Why did you do that, Sam?" his mother asked, genuinely curious.

"Because I want to be in a wedding, too," Sam explained.

Katherine Krupnik stared at him. He was wearing drooping jeans, a dirty sweatshirt with a picture of Goofy on it, and bright red sneakers. There were grape juice stains around his mouth.

"You want to be in a wedding," Mrs. Krupnik said, puzzled.

Anastasia sighed. "It's my fault. I was telling him all about Kirsten's wedding, and how I get to walk down the aisle in my beautiful dress and everything, and have my name in the newspaper, and he said *he* wanted to be a bridesmaid, and I told him —"

Sam interrupted. "She said I couldn't because I'm a boy, and a boy can't be a *maid*, and the only way a boy can be in a wedding is if he's a —"

Mrs. Krupnik nodded. "I get it," she said. "A boy has to be a —"

"Yeah," Anastasia said. "A boy can only be a —"

"*Ringbearer!*" they all said together.

BRRRRINNNG! Sam rang the bell again.

"Make him stop!" Anastasia wailed.

Mrs. Krupnik sighed and looked at the half-finished drawing on her paper. She began to wipe the ink off her pen with a piece of cloth. Then she looked at her children, who were glaring at each other.

"Sometimes," she said, almost to herself, "I wonder what my life would have been like if I'd opted for a full-time career instead of marriage."

"I'm doing just that," Anastasia reminded her. "Renouncing marriage. By the way, Mom, do you know what a sloop is?"

Mrs. Krupnik screwed the lid tightly onto the jar of ink. "A sloop is a kind of boat," she said. She gazed fondly at Sam, who was sucking the thumb of his right hand while he turned the bell over in his left and examined its bottom.

"You know, Anastasia, you renounce a whole lot of good stuff when you renounce marriage," she said.

"Like what?"

"Well, just for starters, a wedding. Your dad and I had a really neat wedding."

Anastasia shrugged. "I get to be in other people's weddings. Like Kirsten Halberg's. I get to walk down the aisle and be in the newspaper and all that, and go to the reception and everything, but I don't have to write all those thank-you notes. Kirsten Halberg already has to say thank you for seven woks."

Sam looked up from his bell. "Wok, wok, wok, wok, wok, wok, wok," he said. "That's seven woks."

"And it's still four and a half weeks to her wedding. Can you imagine how many woks she may end up with? And have to write thank-you notes for?"

Mrs. Krupnik shuddered. "That certainly is something to be considered," she acknowledged. "Your dad and I didn't get a single wok when we got married. We got twelve pairs of silver candlesticks, though."

"I won't ever have that problem," Anastasia told her with satisfaction. "What do you mean, a boat?

What kind of boat is a sloop?"

"Well," her mother said dubiously as she got up from her chair, "bear in mind that you will also be renouncing the fun of having childr—— Sam! Don't you dare!" Sam had put his tricycle bell down on the drawing table and had picked up his mother's little pot of ink.

He looked at her very innocently, still holding the ink.

"Put that down right *now*, Sam," Mrs. Krupnik said. "Right this minute."

Sam backed away from the table, still holding the ink.

"I mean it, Sam," said his mother.

Anastasia watched with interest as her brother and her mother glared at each other. Sam wasn't terribly naughty terribly often, but every now and then, when he got that defiant look in his eyes, which he had right now, it meant trouble.

Sam backed slowly across the broad room, watching his mother. He passed the ink back and forth between his hands.

"BRING THAT TO ME NOW, SAM," Mrs. Krupnik said loudly and firmly.

Sam grinned. He turned and ran from the room, still carrying the ink. "You can't catch me!" he called.

"You were talking about the fun of having children, Mom," Anastasia reminded her. "What kind of boat is a sloop?"

"Go get your brother," Mrs. Krupnik said angrily.

"If he spills that on the living room carpet —"

"Why do I have to go after him? It's not *my* ink,"
Anastasia complained.

"*Anastasia*," Mrs. Krupnik said.

"Anyway, I've given up chasing boys. That ought
to include my brother." Anastasia was arguing, but
she was already starting across the room, because she
could see that her mother wasn't kidding. Far off, in
another part of the house, she could hear Sam chant-
ing, "Wok, wok, wok."

"Go get him. And earn your nickname," her mother
ordered. "*Swifty*."

*

"It won't come off, Sam. You're going to have ink
on your hands for the rest of your life. And that may
not bother you *now*, when you're three years old, but
believe me, you're going to feel a little funny about it
when you're forty. *Then* you'll be sorry."

Anastasia could hear her mother's voice coming
from the bathroom, where she was scrubbing Sam.
They had finally caught him and retrieved the ink on
the second floor, in his bedroom. So the living room
carpet was spared. But there was ink on Sam's hands
and sweatshirt.

Anastasia put the tricycle bell on the table beside
Sam's bed and wandered into the bathroom.

"You never said what a sloop is, exactly," she reminded her mother.

"Oh, for heaven's sake," her mother said in an
impatient voice. She glanced toward the bathtub.

"There. See that red boat of Sam's? Single mast, two sails? That's a sloop."

"Sloop, sloop, sloop," Sam sang, mooshing his hands in the soapy water.

"Quit wiggling," his mother said. "You're going to stay right here until we get that ink off."

"*Sam* has a sloop?" Anastasia asked. She picked up the red boat from the corner rim of the bathtub.

"He's had it for ages. How long have you had that boat, Sam?" Mrs. Krupnik asked.

"Twelve years," Sam replied cheerfully. "No, a *hundred* and twelve years."

"You're probably tired of it," Anastasia said, an idea forming in her mind. "Would you trade it for something?"

Sam stood still, his hands dangling in the basin full of soapy water, and thought. "Trade it for what?" he asked.

Anastasia remembered the one thing that Sam had wanted for a very long time, the one thing that she had always said a very firm no to.

"Sam," she told her brother solemnly, "if you give me your sloop, I will let you take Frank Goldfish into the bathtub with you for one bath. No soap allowed. Just clear water. And no grabbing at Frank, either. Just quiet swimming."

Sam looked at her with wide eyes. "You will? I can?"

"If you give me your sloop."

"Take it. You can have it."

As she went back to her own bedroom, holding the small red wooden boat, Anastasia felt a little ambivalent, a little guilty. It was a pretty terrible burden to place on Frank Goldfish, who was so accustomed to his small bowl and would very likely feel terrified in the bathtub. But Frank was tough. Frank could take it, she was quite sure.

And, after all, it was worth it, Anastasia thought. Because now she was legitimately a woman who owned her own sloop.

Dear Septimus Smith,

I will send you a photograph soon. In my next letter.

I know you got a lot of mail so just to remind you, I am the one who wrote you three letters already. This makes four. I will send a photograph in my fifth letter.

But the thing I wanted to tell you right away is that, even though I am not the woman who you are very interested in who has her own sloop, I am — ta DA! — *also* a woman who has her own sloop.

The reason I didn't tell you before is because I just *got* my sloop. So mine is newer than the woman who already wrote. Well, that's not entirely true, because I have to be honest and tell you that what I got is a *used* sloop.

Still, I thought you might be interested in knowing about my sloop, especially since I live near Boston and not in Sitka, Alaska.

Please write soon, now that you know I have a sloop.

> Sincerely,
> SWIFTY

(Sloop-owner Writing Increasingly Frequently To You)

6

"Frank?" It was Saturday morning, and Anastasia was whispering in a solicitous voice toward the side of the goldfish bowl. "Look at me, Frank. Please accept my very humble apology. I'm truly sorry."

But Frank aimed his tail in her direction and swam listlessly to the opposite side of the bowl.

Sam, kneeling on the rug beside his sister, said in a small voice, "I didn't mean to sit on him in the bathtub. But I was all slithery. Is he okay?"

"I think so. He's just mad, I think."

"He didn't completely squish or anything. I just sat on him for one weensy second."

Anastasia sighed and tapped a little fish food into the bowl. "I think he'll be okay, Sam," she said.

"We'll leave him alone for a while. I think his feelings are hurt. When my feelings are hurt, I just need to be by myself for a while."

"Yeah, me too," Sam said. "My feelings are hurting right now because I mashed Frank. My feelings are hurting very, very bad."

Anastasia put her arm around Sam's skinny shoulders. "It was my fault, really," she told her brother. "I shouldn't have let you take Frank in the tub. But I needed your sloop."

"Yeah." Sam's voice was dejected. "Now I don't have a sloop. And I had a terrible time in the bathtub. And Frank is mashed. Three bad things in a row." He held up three fingers and looked at them mournfully.

Then he gazed at his sister with a sad, pleading look. "Can I have my sloop back?" he asked.

"Nope. I traded for it fair and square."

"I'll give you ten pennies," Sam suggested.

"Sorry. No deal. Life is hard sometimes, Sam," Anastasia told him.

Sam sighed. "Life is hard," he agreed. "I guess I'd better go eat a banana."

"A banana?" Anastasia looked at him, puzzled.

Sam headed for the stairs. "Yeah," he said. "Eat a banana and watch cartoons. That's what I do when life is hard."

"Anastasia?" her mother called from the hallway below. "Your friends are here. Do you want to come down or shall I send them up?"

"Send them up," Anastasia called back. Then she

leaned over the staircase railing and watched Sonya, Meredith, and Daphne climbing the stairs toward her room.

"Hi, guys," she said. "What's the big problem?" Meredith had called earlier and announced that there was a humungous problem that the four of them needed to deal with.

All three of her friends kicked their shoes off automatically. Anastasia was already in her stocking feet. Meredith settled herself on the floor, and Sonya and Daphne sprawled on Anastasia's unmade bed. Anastasia sat backwards on her desk chair, her arms folded over the top of its back. She felt like a hard-bitten detective when she sat that way.

"You have to speak softly," she added, glancing at the fishbowl. "Frank has had a traumatic day and he needs peace and quiet."

"What happened?" Daphne asked. "How can a fish have a traumatic day?"

Anastasia shook her head. "Don't ask. It was awful. Does he look *flat* to you?"

They all gazed at the goldfish for a moment. "Yeah, he looks flat," Sonya said at last. "But he always *was* flat. I don't think he's changed any."

"Good," Anastasia said. "Maybe he's okay, then. What's the big problem, Meredith?"

"Well, first there's just a small problem," Meredith said. "A decision. Which of these do you like best?" She reached into the pocket of her jeans, pulled out three squashed-looking pink things, and tossed them onto Anastasia's desk. Sonya, Daphne, and Anastasia all stared at them.

"Yuck," Daphne said after a moment. "What *are* they?"

Meredith had been taking off her sweater. She glanced over and giggled. "Oh," she said. "They got squooshed."

Anastasia cringed and looked quickly at her goldfish to see if he had heard the word, but Frank seemed to be daydreaming.

Meredith picked up the three pink things and fluffed them out a bit. "*Now* look," she said. "They're fake flowers. We're going to have real ones at the wedding, but these are just so you can vote for which kind you like the best, to carry for your bouquet. What would look best with our dresses? This one's a rose." She held up a wrinkled pink silk rose on a green wire stem.

"And this is a snapdragon." She held up a longer, deeper pink silk flower.

"And this one is a tulip. What do you think? They'll all look better when they're real, my mom says."

"Why *pink*?" Sonya wailed. "Do they have to be pink? I told Kirsten I can't wear pink with my red hair!"

"You won't be *wearing* them," Meredith pointed out. "You hold them down at your waist. They won't be anywhere near your hair."

"Well," Sonya said grudgingly, "I like the roses."

"Tulips are more dramatic," Daphne said. "I want

to look dramatic."

"I vote for snapdragons," Anastasia said. "Snapdragons are neat. You can snap them open and closed; my mom showed me when I was just a little kid."

Meredith sighed. "I knew this wouldn't be easy," she said. She held the three silk flowers in her hand and looked down at them with a frown. "Hey, look!" she said suddenly. "They look good all together."

The other girls nodded. "Can't we have all of them?" Sonya asked. "They call that a mixed bouquet."

"Great idea," Meredith said. "Is that a unanimous vote for a mixed bouquet?"

Everyone nodded, and Meredith dropped the flowers back on Anastasia's desk. "Now for the *tough* decision," she announced.

"Do you have anything to eat? Nonfattening?" Sonya asked. "I always need food when I discuss problems. Just last night my mother called a family meeting to discuss Lack of Help around This House, and it took two tunafish sandwiches for me to get through it.

"Sorry, Frank," she added apologetically, looking at the fishbowl. "Next time I'll have egg salad."

Anastasia handed her the open box of Ritz crackers that was next to the sloop on the windowsill beside her desk.

"Ready?" Meredith asked.

Sonya scooped a handful of crackers out of the box and offered them to the other girls. Everyone shook their heads no. "Okay. Ready," Sonya said, and nibbled at a cracker.

"Well, here's the deal. We have a moral decision to make," Meredith announced.

Anastasia, Sonya, and Daphne all stared at her.

"I'm against capital punishment," Daphne said firmly. "Even though I disagree with my parents on just about everything else, I agree with them on *that*."

Sonya frowned. "About abortion?" she said. "I think I agree with a woman's right to make her own decision, but sometimes I —"

Meredith interrupted. "No, no, nothing like that," she said loudly.

"Shhhh," Anastasia said, and gestured meaningfully toward the goldfish bowl. "Quieter."

"Oh. Sorry, Frank." Meredith lowered her voice. "It's nothing like that. Not a political issue. It has to do with the wedding."

"I won't wear falsies," Anastasia said quickly and firmly. "Absolutely not. I *know* it might make the dress fit better, but it would be *fake*, and I won't do it."

"I will," Daphne said. "I think it'd be neat to wear falsies. Remember, Anastasia, the time you stuffed pantyhouse into a bra, and —"

Anastasia blushed, and all four of them giggled. Frank flicked his tail in disdain.

"It's not about falsies," Meredith explained. "It's about *boys*."

"Boys?"

"Yeah, the opposite sex, the one we renounced, remember?"

"What about them?" Anastasia asked. She wondered for a second whether the mail had arrived yet. Not that the mail had anything to do with *boys*.

"Well, last night we — me, my mom, and Kirsten — were addressing wedding invitations. They made me promise to use my very best handwriting before they let me do any."

"You have pretty good handwriting, Mer," Anastasia remarked. "Mine stinks. Mr. Rafferty made me rewrite my whole entire paper on *Johnny Tremain* because he couldn't read my handwriting."

"Yeah, I know. Yours is awful. Mine's not so bad, though. Anyway, we were doing the invitations last night. I did the ones for your families. We put Sam in, Anastasia, so he's invited, too. But we only did your parents, Sonya. You have too many brothers."

"That's okay," Sonya said, munching on a cracker. "I hate my brothers, anyway."

"You didn't invite my mom and dad together, did you?" Daphne asked in a horrified voice. "They don't even *speak* to each other since they got divorced."

Meredith shook her head. "Of course not, stupid," she said. "Your dad's the minister. He's *doing* the wedding. What do they call it? He's performing the wedding."

"Officiating," Daphne said.

"Right. He's officiating. So we didn't send him an invitation since he'll automatically be there. I addressed one to your mom, though."

Daphne rolled her eyes. "She won't come. Not if my dad's there. If that's the moral question, forget it. She won't come."

"If you'd just let me finish, please?"

"Sorry. I know she won't come, though." Daphne reached over and took a Ritz cracker from the box on Sonya's lap.

"Here's the moral question," Meredith said in a serious voice.

The other three girls were all silent, waiting.

"There are four invitations set aside, not addressed yet. There'll be dancing at the reception, and my mom thought we'd each like to invite a, well, a you-know-what."

"A boy," Sonya said. "Like Norman Berkowitz."

"A boy," Daphne said. "Like Eddie Cox."

"A boy," Anastasia said. "Like Steve Harvey."

"Yeah," Meredith acknowledged. "A boy. Like Kirby McEvedy."

They all sighed and were silent.

"We did give them up, you know," Sonya said.

In a slow, thoughtful voice, Anastasia pointed out, "We only gave up *chasing* them."

"This wouldn't be chasing them, would it?" Daphne asked. "Sending an invitation wouldn't be *chasing*, exactly."

"Well, that's what I thought," Meredith explained. "But I wanted to check with you guys. We *will* need someone to dance with. I don't want to end up dancing with my father and my grandfather."

"I sure don't want to dance with *Sam,*" Anastasia said.

"This is a toughie," Sonya said in a serious voice. She reached into the box for another cracker. "Rats. It's empty already."

Anastasia twisted around in her chair, reached into a desk drawer, and handed Sonya an open box of animal crackers. "Sam left these here," she said. "He ate all the elephants."

"Thanks." Sonya tossed the empty Ritz box into the large wastebasket and started on the animal crackers. "Will there be any other guys there? People we could dance with?" she asked.

Meredith shook her head. "Just old guys," she said. "Friends of Kirsten and Jeff. And my uncle Tim is coming from out of town, to be an usher — he's real good-looking. But he's old, too. He finished college already."

"Well," Daphne said slowly. "It looks to me as if we have to make a sacrifice here."

"Sacrifice dancing? Not dance at all, at a wedding reception, with a live band, and we have those terrific dresses?" Sonya wailed.

"No, you idiot. I meant sacrifice our principles, just for one day," Daphne explained.

"I agree," Anastasia said. "It wouldn't be chasing. And it would help out the wedding, after all, so that if won't be a flop. We wouldn't want Meredith's family to have a flop of a wedding."

Meredith nodded. "Sonya?" she asked. "I don't want to do it unless it's unanimous."

Sonya sighed. "Okay," she said after a moment. "Let's invite them. Norman's address is —"

"I know Norman's address," Meredith said. She reached down to her pocketbook on the floor and pulled out a group of stamped, addressed envelopes held together by a rubber band. "Here they are. I lied when I said they weren't addressed yet."

Sonya began to laugh. She crumpled the empty box of animal crackers and tossed it at Meredith. "I'm starving," she said. "Moral decisions are very appetite-producing. Do you have anything else to eat, Anastasia? Nonfattening?"

Anastasia stood up and stretched. "Not up here," she said. "But let's go downstairs and get some bananas and watch cartoons."

*

Later, after her friends had gone home, Anastasia thought about Septimus Smith and the letter she had mailed to him a few days earlier. She wondered if he would think her pushy, bragging about the sloop. Of course he was very *interested* in sloops, so she had needed to tell him about hers. But still, she hadn't wanted to come across as overeager or anything.

She remembered an article she had read in *Cosmopolitan*. "Keep Him Guessing" it was called. Would Septimus Smith be guessing about her? Wondering whether she was interested in pursuing a relationship with him? The *Cosmo* article had made it quite clear that you should keep your man slightly mystified at all times, wondering whether he is really number one on your list. The article had even suggested little hints for doing that, like sending yourself fabulous bouquets of flowers with cryptic little notes saying things like "Thanks for last night" or simply "Love from You-Know Who." Then the man in your life would see the flowers in your apartment, placed in a conspicuous place (the article had suggested on an occasional table, near the wine rack), but he wouldn't have the bad taste to *ask* about them — he would just *wonder*. It had also suggested hanging a masculine-looking tooth-brush next to your own, in the bathroom.

But Anastasia realized that none of those things would keep Septimus Smith on his toes at all. She didn't have an occasional table; she didn't even know what an occasional table was. (A table that was there one day but not the next, so it was there only *occasionally*? That seemed totally weird.)

She didn't have a wine rack.

She couldn't afford flowers. And anyway, if she sent herself flowers, Septimus Smith wouldn't see them. She could *mention* in a letter that someone had sent her flowers, maybe.

Should she also mention that there was a masculine-looking toothbrush hanging next to hers in the bathroom? She didn't want to *lie*. Of course, she could go and get a masculine-looking toothbrush, hang it there, and *then* mention it in a letter. But it would look stupid, hanging there next to Sam's little yellow toothbrush with the Mickey Mouse head on the end of it. And her parents would ask whose masculine-looking toothbrush the new one was. Anyway, it would be hard to fit a paragraph about toothbrushes into a letter unless, of course, you had a reason to be talking about dental hygiene, and Anastasia couldn't think of one reason in the world to talk to anybody *ever* about dental hygiene. She even got bored when her own dentist, Dr. Dana, reminded her about flossing.

But she did, Anastasia realized, need to keep Septimus on his toes. And now, after her friends' visit, she thought she knew of a way. She pushed the three forgotten pink silk flowers to the corner of her desk, took out a piece of stationery, and began to write.

Dear Septimus,

    I know you have not had a chance to answer my last letter, the one I wrote to tell you that I got a sloop. And of course since you have already had the problem of answering 416 letters, which required a computer since you didn't want to take a day off of work (what kind of work do you do, anyway?), I don't want to add to your burden of correspondence.

    So you can just consider this page 2 of the letter I sent you the other day, the one about the sloop.

    I just wanted to mention that if I should happen to receive a letter from you the first week in May, I will not be able to answer it for a few days. I am usually very prompt at answering my mail, but I will be very busy the first week in May with social events. In fact I recently had to go shopping for a fabulous gown which I will be wearing the first week in May.

    I just happened to think of it while I was sitting here at my occasional table, admiring some flowers I received today.

Sincerely,
SWIFTY

(Sloop-owner With Innumerable Flowers: Tall, Young)

7

"I have to tell you, Anastasia, that Steve Harvey is a creep," Meredith muttered during homeroom. "Even if you *do* like him."

Anastasia shrugged. "I don't *love* him or anything," she whispered. "And I know he's a creep sometimes. But so are all the seventh-grade boys. Why is Steve any creepier than anyone else?"

"His mother called my mother last night," Meredith explained. "And she said that Steve doesn't want to come to the wedding if it means he has to wear a necktie. *Creep.*"

Anastasia groaned. But she couldn't say anything else because the teacher was glaring at them both. They were supposed to be filling out a form from the

Guidance Department.

NAME. First Middle Last. Anastasia Krupnik, she penciled in carefully, leaving "Middle" blank. Sometimes she wished that her parents had given her a middle name. She knew that across the aisle Meredith was writing "Anne" in that space. Anastasia Anne Krupnik wouldn't be bad at all.

Up in the front seat, Sonya would be writing "Sophia" in the middle-name space. Rats. To have no middle name was *so* boring.

Anastasia went on to the next line and printed her address and telephone number. She wondered why the Guidance Department needed that — surely they would never call her at home. She pictured herself answering the telephone and hearing a voice say, "Hello, this is the Guidance Department." Talk about gross.

SEX. She made a capital F, to indicate Female, which should have been perfectly obvious, since her name was Anastasia. The only person in the seventh grade who might possibly have presented a problem would be Jamie Seaver, who was female, but who *could* be a male Jamie, except that Jamie Seaver's middle name was Elizabeth, for Pete's sake, and the Guidance Department would *see* that, because Jamie would have written "Elizabeth" in the middle-name space.

To have a line for SEX there was so idiotic. The only thing it produced was a lot of boys snickering — as they were doing right now, right this minute; Anastasia could hear them — as they wrote in the word "Often" instead of M for Male.

Seventh-grade boys *were* immature creeps, she thought, and especially Steve Harvey. She wondered what would happen about the necktie. She did want him to come to the wedding, even if he was a creep, because she needed someone to dance with.

The teacher had looked away, so Anastasia whispered across the aisle to Meredith, "What did your mom tell Mrs. Harvey?"

Meredith wrote something quickly on a slip of paper and held it up so that Anastasia could see.

TURTLENECKS OK, it said. HE'S COMING.

Later, in the hall on their way to gym class, Meredith said, "All four of them are coming together: Steve, Kirby, Eddie, and Norman. They're all going to wear turtlenecks except Norman." Meredith giggled. "Norman Berkowitz *likes* wearing neckties!"

*

Sam appeared, wearing his pajamas, in the doorway of Anastasia's bedroom that evening.

"I had a very terrible bath just a few minutes ago," he announced in a disconsolate voice.

"How come?"

"No sloop."

"Oh. Well, sorry about that." Anastasia glanced at the toy sloop, which still sat on her windowsill.

Sam sighed. "If I open up my GI Joe bank, I can give you twenty-five pennies," he suggested. "Would you give me back my sloop for —"

"*My* sloop," his sister corrected.

His face fell. "Would you give me your sloop for twenty-five pennies?" he asked.

"Nope. It's not for sale. I need it."

Sam put his thumb into his mouth. He eyed the sloop sadly. Finally, pouting, he turned and trudged back down the stairs.

Anastasia opened her closet door and looked at the beautiful blue dress hanging there. She wondered if she would be truly beautiful herself, for the first time, when she was wearing the dress, carrying the bouquet of pink flowers, and walking down the aisle of the Congregational church.

There had been times in the past when Anastasia had thought: *Now*. Now is the time I am going to be beautiful. Then she had had a new haircut or something and looked in the mirror afterward, and it hadn't happened.

Her parents both said that they thought she was beautiful already. But parents *always* said that to their kids, so their opinions weren't trustworthy on that particular issue.

Thinking about beauty made Anastasia think of her promise to send Septimus a photograph. She groaned to herself and pulled open the top drawer of her desk, the drawer where she kept important junk.

Her mother had an Important Junk drawer in the kitchen. It was filled with bits of string, thumbtacks, receipts from the dry cleaner, warranty papers from the microwave and the Cuisinart, and recipes torn out of magazines (Anastasia had secretly thrown away the one for Chicken Livers Supreme).

Anastasia's Important Junk drawer was very different from her mother's. There was a deck of cards. Anastasia never played cards, but someone had pointed out to her that in this particular deck, the queens looked a lot like Anastasia, though they weren't wearing glasses.

She looked fondly at the queen of hearts. Then she sorted through the whole deck and tossed all the cards except the queens and kings (Sam called them the Qs and Ks) into her wastebasket. She really liked looking at the queens and picturing herself with contact lenses and fancy headgear. As for the kings — well, you never knew. They certainly didn't look at all like Steve Harvey, who had freckles and somewhat shaggy hair, not at all like the long, carefully curled hair of the kings. But they were quite handsome and might just be an omen of someone in her future.

Maybe even Septimus Smith.

She put a rubber band around the eight Qs and Ks and returned them to the drawer.

She pulled out a crumpled piece of notebook paper and reread an essay she had once written for school. The assignment had been to write something called "Turning Point," about a time in her life which had been just that: a turning point. She had written about the birth of her brother and the death of her grandmother; both things had happened the same day, when Anastasia was ten.

Mr. Rafferty had given her an A+ for "Turning Point"; and Mr. Rafferty didn't give many A+'s, certainly not to Anastasia Krupnik. She had intended to frame the essay but somehow had never gotten around to it, because frames cost so much. But she thought she would probably keep it forever so that her children could read it someday.

She folded "Turning Point" carefully and replaced it in the drawer.

In the bottom was a collection of photographs. She spread them across her desk, stared at them, and sighed.

Anastasia, age twelve, sticking her tongue out at the camera. No way could she send that to Septimus Smith.

Anastasia, age eleven, dressed for Halloween with a stupid bright red wig on her head, a dumb checkered dress with a pinafore over it, and striped tights. Raggedy Ann. Gross. Someone named Septimus Smith had probably never even *heard* of Raggedy Ann. She pushed the photograph aside and picked up another.

Anastasia just last month, grinning into the camera and holding Daphne's cat. She looked at it carefully and decided she didn't look *too* bad, though she was wearing a sweatshirt that said CHARGE! across the front, with a picture of a MasterCard beneath the letters.

She made a face and set it aside. She didn't want Septimus Smith to think that she was into shopping.

She didn't even *like* shopping, except at yard sales, where you could sometimes get neat stuff for a dollar.

Anastasia swept the group of snapshots back into the drawer and went downstairs.

Sam was already in bed, and her parents were in the living room. Her father was reading the newspaper, and her mother was sewing a patch on the knee of Sam's blue jeans.

"May I look at the photograph album?" Anastasia asked.

"Sure," her mother said. "You don't need to ask permission for stuff like that. It's on the bottom shelf beside the fireplace, in the study."

Anastasia brought the dark green leather album back to the living room, sprawled on the floor, and began to turn the pages from the back to the front. Her father glanced over. "I wonder why we always look at some things backwards," he commented. "I always leaf through *Time* magazine from back to front."

"It would be the right direction if we were Japanese," Anastasia pointed out. "I wonder if Japanese people read *Time* magazine from front to back."

"Well," said her father, wrinkling his nose to adjust his glasses, "we'll have to ask a Japanese person sometime." He looked back down at the *Boston Globe*.

"I read some things in little jumps," Mrs. Krupnik said.

Anastasia's father looked up again. *"Little jumps?"* he asked.

Mrs. Krupnik nodded. "Like *War and Peace*," she explained. "I only read the peace parts. I jumped from one peace part to the next. I never read the war parts."

Myron Krupnik put his newspaper down on the coffee table. It was extremely rare for him to put the *Boston Globe* down once he had picked it up. He stared at his wife. "You never read the war parts in *War and Peace?*" he asked in amazement.

She smiled and turned the leg of Sam's jeans around so that she could start on the next side of the patch. "No," she said. "I hate war parts."

"Me too," Anastasia said. "I hate war parts. I skipped the war parts in *Johnny Tremain.* Look, you guys, here's a nudie picture of Sam having a bath when he was two."

"Isn't that sweet?" Mrs. Krupnik said affectionately, leaning over to see.

Anastasia's father rolled his eyes. "I can't believe that you two —" he began.

"Oh, look at this!" Anastasia exclaimed. "I love this picture of me because I look like a werewolf. See how the flash gave me red eyeballs? Just like a werewolf."

Her mother chuckled, and her father picked up the newspaper again with a sigh.

I can't send Septimus Smith a werewolf picture, Anastasia thought. She turned the pages slowly backward through the album. There was Sam, wrapped in a blanket, the day they brought him home from the hospital after he was born.

There was her mother, pregnant with Sam, laughing and pointing at her own big belly. Anastasia peered intently at her mother's face in that photograph. Weird. Her mother looked like *her*, only older, of course, and pregnant.

What she *wanted* was a picture of herself looking mature. Her mother's face was exactly right. Maybe she could — no. Septimus Smith definitely would not be thrilled with a picture of a pregnant lady.

She flipped the pages again.

"I think I look pretty mature in this picture, don't you?" She pointed to a snapshot of herself with her hair gathered up into a bun on the top of her head.

Her mother looked. "Yeah. With your hair up that way, you looked very mature for an eight-year-old. You looked at least nine."

At least *nine. Great.* Anastasia pictured Septimus Smith looking intently at the snapshot and thinking, Wow. Swifty looks at least nine. I think I'll invite her to the Caribbean for a week.

As she continued turning pages, she grew younger and younger, smaller and smaller, in the photographs. It was a lost cause. There was no photograph that she could send to Septimus. Their relationship would end for Lack of Photograph. *Cosmopolitan* had occasionally given lists of reasons for relationships' ending: lack of love, lack of rapport, lack of honesty, lack of *money*, even. But they had never mentioned Lack of Photograph.

Now she was absent from the photographs entirely.

71

She was back on the pages before she was born.

Here was another photograph, suddenly, of her mother's face looking like hers, but older and more mature. Maybe she could — no. It was a wedding picture. She couldn't send a wedding picture to Septimus.

A few loose photographs, not glued to pages, fluttered into her lap. She picked one up and looked at it, startled.

"Wow, look at this," she said to her mother.

Her mother glanced over and smiled. "That was the day I graduated from art school," she said. "I was twenty-two."

Anastasia studied the photograph of her mother at twenty-two. It was the face, she realized, that *she* would probably have at twenty-two. No glasses. By then, Anastasia was certain, her parents would let her get contacts.

Long hair, but not messy like Anastasia's hair.

A lovely smile, and beautiful teeth.

Anastasia ran her tongue over her own teeth. Maybe I *will* floss, she thought. Any day now. Before I'm twenty-two.

"This isn't glued in," she pointed out. "Can I have it?"

"May," her father said.

"*May* I have it?" Anastasia said patiently.

"Sure," her mother replied. "Just don't draw a mustache on it."

"*Mom*," Anastasia said, "I wouldn't dream of doing an immature thing like that."

She returned the album to the bookshelf and took the single photograph to her room. Sitting at her desk again, she stared at the lovely face that *could* be her own in nine years.

She took out a fresh sheet of stationery.

But she hesitated. It would be a lie. She didn't really want a relationship based on a lie. But —

Anastasia took out the one letter she had received from Septimus Smith. He sure isn't much of a correspondent, she thought. I've written him *twice* since I got this one, and he hasn't answered yet.

But maybe he's waiting for the photograph. Maybe he'll *never* write if I don't send a photograph.

She fingered the photograph of her mother tentatively.

But I've never been a liar, she reminded herself.

Slowly she reread his computer-written letter. And suddenly she realized something. He hadn't said, "PLEASE SEND A PHOTOGRAPH OF YOUR-SELF."

He had simply said, "PLEASE SEND A PHOTO-GRAPH."

So that's what she would do. And it wouldn't be a lie at all.

Dear Septimus,

Please consider this page 3 of the letter I have already sent in two parts. I don't want you to think I am overdoing the correspondence.

You said in your letter to please send a photograph.

Enclosed is a photograph.

Sincerely,
SWIFTY

(So: What Is Forthcoming To Yours-truly?)

8

Two weeks before Kirsten Halberg's wedding, everything began going wrong for everybody.

Kirsten announced on Tuesday that she was thinking of calling the whole marriage off because she had
just discovered, when they went to get the marriage
license, that her fiancé's middle name was Neptune.
There was no *way*, she said furiously, that she could
be married to someone whose name was *Neptune*.
What were they supposed to do: name their kids after
planets? Was she going to have a son named Pluto?

Anastasia agreed with her completely, though she
couldn't understand why someone would get involved
with someone else romantically without knowing that
person's middle name. She herself planned to ask

Septimus his middle name the minute their relationship began to jell.

But she was desolate, for the two days that Kirsten's fury lasted, thinking of a called-off wedding, thinking of her beautiful gown unworn.

On Thursday Kirsten grouchily announced that she would marry Jeff anyway if he promised never to *use* his middle name. And no planet babies.

On Friday Sam announced that he would not go to the wedding unless he could wear blue jeans. Mrs. Krupnik said absolutely not; he would wear his white sailor suit. Sometimes before she had talked him into the sailor suit by pointing out that it made him look like Popeye.

Finally Sam said grouchily that he would wear the white sailor suit if he could have a ballpoint pen tattoo of an anchor on his arm.

Mrs. Krupnik said yes, and told Sam that she would even do a three-color tattoo for him. So Sam agreed, and Mrs. Krupnik whispered to Anastasia and her father that fortunately Sam had forgotten that the sailor suit had long sleeves.

"But I won't take a bath before the wedding," Sam added. "Not unless Anastasia sells me the sloop."

"Anastasia?" Mrs. Krupnik gave her a questioning look.

"Nope."

"I'll give you *fifty* pennies!" Sam wailed.

"No sloop. Sorry," Anastasia told him. "I'll consider renting it to you for a day, but that's the best I can do."

On Saturday Daphne's mother, Caroline Bellingham, announced, as Daphne had predicted, that she would not attend the wedding because *that man* would be there. *That man* was John Bellingham, her ex-husband, Daphne's father.

Mrs. Halberg talked to Mrs. Bellingham very tactfully and explained that Reverend Bellingham would be there only in his official capacity, not as an invited guest.

Finally Mrs. Bellingham agreed to go, but only if *that woman* were not invited.

"Who's *that woman?*" Anastasia asked Daphne with interest. The four girls were at Sonya's house on Saturday afternoon, talking about hair styles for the wedding.

"You know, the woman my dad's dating. Her name's Frances Bidwell. She's in the church choir."

"So my mom assured her that Frances Bidwell wasn't on the list of invited guests," Meredith explained.

"But," she added guiltily, "what she *didn't* tell her is that Frances Bidwell is going to be in the church balcony, singing a solo right in the middle of the wedding. Don't you dare tell her, Daphne."

Daphne giggled. "I won't. But she'll probably freak when Frances Bidwell stands up."

Word had gotten out that Steve, Eddie, Norman, and Kirby were planning to bring skateboards to the wedding reception. So there had been a conference with Steve, Eddie, Norman, and Kirby's parents; now the skateboards were forbidden.

"That's *so* immature," Sonya had said, shaking her head. "I don't know how I ever liked Norman Berkowitz."

More presents were arriving daily at the Halberg house, and Mr. Halberg said he was spending every waking minute of every day signing UPS delivery slips for woks, then returning woks to the store they had come from. He was beginning to think that they were getting the *same* wok again and again, as new people bought it every day. Finally they decided to keep all the woks until after the wedding, returning them after Kirsten and Steve had left for their honeymoon.

"Or, of course, we could open a Chinese restaurant," Meredith pointed out.

Sam loved the word "wok." He used it whenever he could. In the evenings Anastasia could hear him in the bathtub, singing, "Wok, wok, wok your boat, gently down the stream . . ."

And he made up wok jokes. Some of them were pretty funny, actually.

"Why did the Chinese guy put a leash on his dog?" Sam asked one afternoon.

"I don't know. Why?"

"So he could take it for a wok! Get it?"

But his family tried to distract Sam from his wok infatuation because Kirsten Halberg said she never wanted to hear the word "wok" again as long as she lived.

"Sam," Mrs. Krupnik said one evening, "it's okay to talk about woks a *little*, here at home. But when we go to the wedding —"

Sam's eyes lit up. He was quite interested in the whole topic of weddings, now that he was going to have an anchor tattoo on his arm. "Why did the Chinese lady have a wedding?" he asked.

Mrs. Krupnik responded with a sigh. "I don't know. Why?"

"So she could wok down the aisle!" shrieked Sam. "Get it? Get it?"

"Sam," said his mother, laughing, "when we're at the wedding, it would be nice if —"

Sam interrupted her. "What did the Chinese lady sing to her baby?" he asked gleefully.

Mrs. Krupnik grinned. " 'Wok-a-bye Baby'?" she asked.

Myron Krupnik and Anastasia both groaned. "You guys are *terrible*," Anastasia said to her mother and brother. "You'd never hear Dad or me telling —"

Her father held his hand up. "Listen! I've got one!" he said with a gleam in his eye. "What kind of music did the Chinese lady like best?"

They all looked at him. No one said anything.

"Wok-and-roll," Myron Krupnik said apologetically. "Sorry. I couldn't help myself."

"Here is what we've decided about hair," Anastasia announced at dinner. "And Kirsten approved."

"Decided about hair?" her father asked, looking mystified.

"For the *wedding*, Dad," Anastasia explained patiently. "For the junior bridesmaids' hair styles."

Myron Krupnik shook his head. "Oh," he said, and went back to his lasagna.

"We're all going to wear it up on top of our heads, Mom," Anastasia explained. "Sonya thought hers wasn't long enough. But we tested it out on everybody over at her house Saturday, and it looked just fine. So it will be up on top of our heads, with a small blue ribbon tied around it."

"Sounds lovely," Mrs. Krupnik said.

"Lovely," Sam said solemnly.

"At first we thought pink ribbons, to match the bouquets. But Sonya just can't bear wearing pink, with her red hair. So we decided on blue."

"Nice. I'm sure it will be just wonderful."

"And the ribbon will have a little streamer down the back so that when we walk down the aisle —"

"*Wok* down the aisle," Sam interrupted.

"Right. When we wok down the aisle, we'll look interesting from the back."

"How shall I wear *my* hair, I wonder. Is it long enough for a ponytail?" Anastasia's father asked. "I certainly want to look interesting from the back." He pulled his shaggy hair away from his bald spot and held it bunched in his hand at the back of his neck.

"*Myron,*" Mrs. Krupnik said in a meaningful voice.

"And guess what! There's a *rehearsal* the day before the wedding, just as if we were going to be in a play. And after the rehearsal, there's a rehearsal *dinner* just for the families and the members of the wedding party. So that includes me!"

"Sounds great, sweetie. Myron, want any more lasagna? Or are you ready for dessert?"

"I'll have some more, thanks. My *first* plate was just a rehearsal dinner. Now for the real thing." He handed his empty plate to his wife.

Anastasia got up to answer the telephone, which was ringing in the kitchen.

"Do you know of any diet that makes you thin in a week and a half?" Sonya asked over the phone. "I just realized that there's only a week and a half till the wedding, and I forgot to go on a diet."

"Can't you ask your father? He's a doctor," Anastasia reminded her.

Sonya groaned. "He'd just make a big speech about the danger of crash diets. He'd make me read brochures about anorexia. I was thinking of maybe calling Oprah Winfrey, though. *She'd* know, don't you think?"

"Yeah, probably she would. But, Sonya —"

"What?"

"If you went on some diet now and lost of lot of weight before the wedding, your *dress* wouldn't fit!"

Sonya was silent for a minute. "I hadn't thought of that," she said.

"And your dress looks terrific the way it is. *You* look terrific in it. You don't need to lose weight."

"You're sure?"

"Positive," Anastasia assured her. "When you walk down the aisle —"

"Wok," Sonya corrected. She sounded, for a moment, like Sam. It was weird, the way they were all automatically incorporating wok into their conversation, Anastasia thought. She laughed.

"Sorry. I meant *wok* down the aisle, of course. You'll look fabulous. Forget the diet idea."

"Okay. I'll go on a diet *after* the wedding. At the reception I'll start."

"Just a week and a half left," Anastasia reminded her happily.

"A wok and a half," Sonya replied, giggling, and hung up.

"By the way, Dad," Anastasia said when she went back to the table, "I know you're sick of hearing about the wedding, but there *is* one truly important detail that Mom may not have told you about yet. And this will definitely interest you."

"What's that?" her father asked politely.

"All of us junior bridesmaids are supposed to wear little pearl earrings. In fact, Kirsten made us each a *gift* of little pearl earrings. Actually, she didn't officially make the gift yet. She's giving them to us at the rehearsal dinner. That's traditional: the bride gives gifts to the bridesmaids at the rehearsal dinner."

Her father looked at her while he chewed slowly on a mouthful of lasagna. Finally, he said, "Well, that certainly is a truly important detail which definitely interests me. It's right up there with — oh, let's say world peace, maybe."

"No, no, Dad," Anastasia went on, laughing. "I know you're not fascinated with pearl earrings. *Here's*

82

the interesting thing. Kirsten bought earrings for pierced ears. Meredith has pierced ears, and Sonya has pierced ears, and Daphne has pierced ears, and I'm the only one who doesn't have pierced ears. *Yet,*" she added meaningfully.

Her father nodded. "And I suspect that you're going to tell me that *that* means —"

"Right!" Anastasia grinned. "Mom said okay. And tomorrow I'm going to get a lobotomy!"

Her father started to laugh. About time, thought Anastasia. About *time* he took an interest in the preparations for the wedding. But what was so *funny*, for Pete's sake?

Then he explained. "Sorry, sport, for laughing. But a lobotomy is a kind of brain surgery."

"Oh," Anastasia said, a little embarrassed. "Well, as far as I'm concerned, lobe-piercing is pretty much the same."

"By the way, Anastasia," Mrs. Krupnik said as she began to clear the dinner plates from the table, "did you check through the mail in the front hall? You got a letter this morning from your pen pal."

Dear Swifty,

I'm sorry it has taken me so long to reply. You can envision, I'm sure, the height of a stack of 416 letters. My computer letter did narrow it down. The lady from Sitka did not respond, of course. Nor did the lady with the Siamese cats. So I had only 414 replies, plus your additional two letters, which made the new stack 416 again.

Now, after reading all of those and looking at 402 photographs (several ladies chose not to send any), I am sending personal letters only to two. And frankly, I chose the two ladies who have sloops. I am very attracted to sloops, I have to confess. Please tell me more about yours.

In addition to your sloop, I find your handwriting interesting. You did not mention your profession. But I am speculating that you may be a doctor. Your handwriting looks very much like that of a doctor.

And your nickname is appealing. What is the origin of "Swifty"? I am guessing that you race. I have participated in the Monhegan and Bermuda races myself, so I think we may have a real interest — or even a passion — in common.

Your location is also advantageous. The other lady who owns a sloop is in California, and Boston is so much closer to New York. I go to Boston fairly often. In fact, I will be there early in May — goodness, a couple of weeks from now — but unfortunately you indicated that your social calendar was full that week, so we will have to meet another time.

Thank you for the photograph. I received all sorts of photographs, including three that could be considered X-rated. I liked yours for its almost old-fashioned quality.

You asked what kind of work I do, and I am a little embarrassed to tell you that I don't work at all. Does that bother you? It takes me a great deal of time simply to manage my portfolio.

I look forward to hearing from you again.

Sincerely,
Septimus Smith

9

"I'm a little bit nervous about this," Anastasia confessed to Daphne as they made their way through the crowds at the shopping mall. Her friend was accompanying her to the large department store where she was to have her ears pierced.

"It's no big deal. It only takes a second, and it doesn't hurt. They use a gun."

Anastasia stopped walking. She stood still in front of a video rental store.

"A *gun?*"

Daphne giggled. "Not a real gun. A special earlobe-gun."

"An earlobe-gun," Anastasia repeated to herself in a dubious voice. "*Great.*" But she started walking again.

"I'm thinking of getting more holes punched in my lobes so I can wear maybe three earrings in each ear. But my mom freaks out when I mention it. She's afraid I'd wear safety pins."

"Would you?" Anastasia asked. Nothing Daphne did would really surprise her.

Daphne shrugged. "I might," she admitted. "Anyway, I don't see why my mom is freaked out by that. *She* has a tattoo."

Anastasia stopped walking again, this time in front of Casual Male. "Daphne," she said. "Gimme a break. No way does your mom have a tattoo. Up until a few months ago she was a minister's wife."

Daphne grinned. "Yeah, she really does. Her dad — my grandfather — was a doctor. And when she was a baby, he thought it would be a really smart thing to have his kids' blood types tattooed on them, in case they were ever in an accident. She has this little teeny blue tattoo on her butt."

"*Gross.*"

"*She* thinks it's gross, too," Daphne went on, "but not because it's a tattoo. Because of her blood type — B negative. They write that like a B minus. And her sister was A plus! Mom says she wouldn't mind having A plus on her behind, but she hates being a B minus!"

"What if she was an F!" Anastasia said.

"You can't be. Blood types are only A, B, AB, and O. We learned that in Science, remember?"

"Yeah. I forgot."

"Come on, Anastasia. There's the store. Let's get

your lobes done, and then we can go to the record store and look at albums."

"Okay." Anastasia headed toward the entrance of Jordan Marsh. She was still a little nervous. Her mother had been, too. She had agreed to the ear-piercing on the condition that Anastasia have it done by a doctor under absolutely sterile conditions. Her mother had read once about an earlobe that had gotten infected and fallen off, or something.

So Anastasia had agreed, and asked her mother to call the doctor for an appointment. Anastasia hated calling doctors. She had had to do it once when her mom was away on business and Sam got chicken pox.

She had sat in the kitchen stirring a marshmallow into a cup of cocoa while her mother called the doctor's office and explained to the receptionist what they wanted.

"What did she say?" she asked her mother after the receptionist replied.

"She's getting the doctor so I can talk to him. Yes? Hello?" She turned back to the telephone and Anastasia listened while her mother explained the whole thing again.

Her mother listened for a minute and then said, "Oh, I see. Well, that's what we'll do, then. Thank you."

She hung up, looked at Anastasia, and shrugged. "He said he doesn't have the slightest idea how to pierce ears and we should go to the jewelry department at Jordan Marsh. They have a special instrument, and it's sterile, and quick, and painless, and inexpensive."

"Why do you look so miserable? Want a sip of my cocoa?"

Her mother nodded and took a sip, which left her with a marshmallow mustache. "I'm embarrassed," she said. "He made me feel dumb."

Anastasia sympathized. "People make me feel dumb all the time," she said. "Here. You can have my whole cup of cocoa. Cocoa always makes people feel better."

"Thank you. Promise me one thing, Anastasia."

"What?"

"You won't get big dangly earrings. Or rhinestones. I can't bear the thought of seeing you with rhinestone earrings."

"I promise," Anastasia had told her.

It turned out to be accurate, what the doctor had said. And what Daphne had said, too. It *was* like a little gun. It was quick, painless, and presumably sterile. ZAP. And: ZAP.

Anastasia looked at herself in the mirror, there at the store, and beamed. She had a little gold stud in each ear. She pictured herself on the following Saturday, when she would replace them with the tiny pearl earrings, put on the beautiful blue dress, and tie the narrow ribbon around her upswept hair.

She wondered for the fiftieth time whether she would qualify, next Saturday, as beautiful.

*

"They're lovely. They don't hurt, do they?" her mother asked.

"Nope. I can't even feel them." Anastasia dropped her hair back down around her ears and leaned over her mother's drawing table, looking at the nearly finished illustration of the farmer and his cows. "Why don't you put earrings on the female cows?"

Her mother studied the picture. The cows were carrying pocketbooks and shopping bags, and several were wearing high-heeled shoes.

"*All* cows are female," she reminded Anastasia. "A male cow is a bull. There's going to be a bull farther along in the book. I was thinking of making him look like Rambo."

Anastasia giggled.

"But I like the idea of earrings. It's not too late to add them. Maybe even rhinestones." She picked up a pen.

Anastasia glanced around the room. Suddenly she was reminded of something.

"Mom? You know that big leather case you use when you take your drawings to the publisher? That one there, against the wall."

Her mother glanced over to where Anastasia was pointing. "My portfolio. What about it?"

Anastasia frowned. "Well, I was just wondering. Do you ever have trouble managing it?"

"Yeah, *lots*. I don't dare check it with my luggage because I'm afraid it might get lost, or bashed around. So I have to carry it on the plane when I go to New York, and it never fits in the overhead compartment.

So the stewardess always gets mad, and has to stick it in with the garment bags, and it holds everybody up. So I'm always apologizing for it. And once I left it in a taxi, and *that* was a big problem, getting it back. Yeah, I guess I'd say I do have a lot of trouble with it."

"But would you say that you have to spend all your time managing it?"

"Good grief, no. It's not that big a deal. Why?"

"Well, I know this person who says he has to spend all his time managing his portfolio. He can't even *work*, because it takes so much of his time, just managing his portfolio. Isn't that kind of weird?"

Mrs. Krupnik put down her pen and began to laugh. "Weird in a very interesting way. He's — did you say it was a he?"

Anastasia nodded.

"Well, he's talking about something different. What he means is that he owns a whole lot of stocks and bonds. That's called a portfolio, but it's a different thing. Someone who has to spend all his time managing that kind of portfolio is very, very rich. Goodness, where did you meet someone like that?"

Anastasia hesitated. "I didn't really meet him," she said. "I just heard about it."

"Well," said her mother, picking up her pen again, "there are a lot of women out there who would love to meet someone like that!"

"Yeah," Anastasia replied. "Like about four hundred and sixteen."

*

Back in her room, Anastasia reread her letter from Septimus Smith. She was awfully glad that her mother had explained the whole portfolio thing. Otherwise she might have written and suggested that he put his portfolio in with the garment bags on airplanes. Then she would have sounded like a jerk, and probably he would never have written to her again, right when their relationship was getting off to a pretty good start.

"Tell me more about your sloop," he had written.

She glanced at the little toy boat she had set on her windowsill. It was made of wood, and it was bright red. She figured she could tell him that. It was also about seven inches long, something she decided not to mention.

"I am guessing that you race," he had said. Anastasia wondered why he was interested in racing. Maybe, when he wasn't busy managing his portfolio, he jogged. She herself was not at all attracted to joggers, mainly because they smelled sweaty all the time. But probably he took showers after he raced.

Anastasia was not really into racing, but she always participated when they had races in gym class. Usually she did well, because she was tall and had long legs. So she could tell Septimus that she raced, and it wouldn't be a lie.

And he thought she was a doctor. She would have to confess to him that she was not. But maybe he wouldn't be disappointed. Doctors always had to wear beepers, and when their beepers went off in restaurants and theaters, people glared at them.

He was going to be in Boston next week. Anastasia had mixed feelings about that. She wanted to meet Septimus Smith sometime, but next week was too soon, so probably it was just as well that he knew her social calendar was full. She wanted to meet him after she was a little older, and had gotten contact lenses, and maybe finished college and all. The pierced ears were a good start — she glanced again in the mirror, thinking about them — but still, next week was too soon for their meeting.

She wondered about the sloop lady in California. California was full of movie stars, Anastasia knew. Still, probably Septimus would have mentioned it if the sloop lady was Debra Winger.

He had narrowed it down to 2, out of 416, and Anastasia was one of them. Much better odds than her seventh-grade class, where she felt fairly certain that Steve Harvey occasionally noticed that Emily Ewing had absolutely perfect hair and that the Wilcox twins had amazingly large bosoms for people thirteen years old.

She took a fresh piece of stationery out of her desk and began to write.

Dear Septimus,

Thank you for your letter!!! I was really thrilled to get it.

I *do* race occasionally. Just last week I raced, and came in second. I have to confess that I am not extremely interested in racing, but I am willing to do it now and then.

I always, of course, take a shower afterward.

About my sloop: it is made of wood, painted red. It has not been in the water for a while, but when it is in the water, the red paint, which is a little faded, looks really neat because it seems darker. I am thinking of putting a fresh coat on it one of these days.

Other people have sometimes commented on my interesting handwriting. Someone named Mr. Rafferty calls it indecipherable. But what does he know, right?

No, I am not a doctor, and therefore I do not ever have to wear a beeper or anything else which might be a nuisance in restaurants or, for that matter, during races.

My profession, which I forgot to mention, is that I am sort of a scholar.

I was interested to hear about your profession. I have a very close relative who has an extremely large portfolio and she sometimes has trouble managing it.

I regret that circumstances make it impossible for us to meet when you are in Boston next week. But anyway, it would be better if our first meeting takes place sometime in the future. I need to complete some scholarly stuff first, and also to have some work done in the area of my eyes.

Perhaps you already know from *People* magazine that Debra Winger has a young son. I have no
children. I like them, of course, but in my current
busy life, being childless is an advantage, I feel.
I am glad that you liked the photograph I sent.

                                        Sincerely,
                                        SWIFTY

(Scholar With Interesting Future: Tall, Young).

10

"Do I look okay?" Anastasia asked anxiously. She turned around, slowly, in the doorway of the living room, where her parents were sitting. They looked over at her and smiled.

Sam looked up from the complicated structure he was building from blocks on the floor. He smiled, too. He and Anastasia were pals again because she had agreed to loan him the sloop, free of charge, for his pre-wedding bath the next day.

"You look wonderful," her mother said. "You really do."

Her father gave her a thumbs-up sign. Sam watched his dad and tried to do the same thing, but he wasn't terribly good at it, and he went back to his skyscraper.

It was the night of the rehearsal and the rehearsal dinner. Anastasia was wearing a yellow dress and a gold necklace to match her new earrings.

They could hear the beep of a car horn in front of the house. Anastasia looked through the window.

"That's Sonya," she said. "Her brother's driving us over. I'll be back around ten."

"Have a wonderful time," her mom said. "And remember, when you practice walking down the aisle —"

"Woking," Sam corrected automatically.

Mrs. Krupnik laughed. "Yes. When you wok down the aisle, stand up straight. Pretend you're in the Miss America contest."

Anastasia made a face and waved goodbye as she went through the front door.

*

The rehearsal was sort of weird. Kristen kept giggling nervously while she stood beside Jeff at the front of the church. Daphne's father, the minister, didn't seem to mind. He told her that all brides were nervous.

Reverend Bellingham didn't actually say the whole ceremony. He just said, "Now I'll do blah blah blah, and Jeff, you take the ring —"

So Jeff took an imaginary ring and pretended to put it on Kirsten's finger while Kirsten giggled self-consciously.

"Then Frances will sing," Reverend Bellingham said. He looked up to the balcony of the church, where Frances Bidwell was standing. "Do you want to go through your song, Frances, or shall we skip it?"

"Let's skip it," Frances called back. "I've sung it a hundred times before. It'll be fine."

"Okay, then Frances sings, blah blah blah. And then," he said, "at the end, I'll say blah blah blah, and you can kiss each other —"

So Jeff and Kirsten both made loud kissing noises into the air while everybody laughed.

"*Then*," Reverend Bellingham went on, "everyone goes back down the aisle and out of the church. You first, Kirsten and Jeff; then the maid of honor with the best man; then the bridesmaids, each one with an usher. You first, Meredith, since you're her sister. You take *this* usher's arm —"

Meredith, looking embarrassed, took Jeff's brother's arm and started down the aisle.

"Then you, Anastasia, you take *this* usher's arm —"

Anastasia, feeling embarrassed, took the arm of Meredith's Uncle Tim. She was secretly glad that she'd been paired with him because he was the handsomest of the ushers, and the tallest, and Meredith had whispered to her that Uncle Tim, who was her mother's youngest brother, led a very glamorous life and drove a Porsche. But he looked just the teensiest bit bored, she thought, at having to march down the aisle with a seventh-grader.

Finally the rehearsal was over, and Reverend Bellingham assured them all that things would be perfect the next day.

"You *promise* that you won't use his middle name," Kirsten said for about the fifteenth time.

Reverend Bellingham, who really was a nice guy even though Daphne's mother said he was a sanctimonious creep, promised for the fifteenth time. He crossed his heart, and just for that moment, crossing his heart, looked like a Catholic, Anastasia thought.

Then they all piled into cars to go to the restaurant where they would have dinner. Anastasia had vowed to herself that she would eat absolutely everything on her plate even if it was something she hated — even if it was chicken livers. She had vowed to be outgoing and to make polite conversation, even with strangers. She had vowed to be poised and interesting and to sit up straight and use the right fork, and not to take a single bite until the person at the head of the table did.

She almost blew it the first minute, after they were all seated at a large table in a private room. She turned to the person on her left — the groom's older brother — and said politely, "I understand you're a lawyer. That's very interes——"

To her surprise, he put his fingers to his lips and said, "Shhhh." Was it a secret that he was a lawyer? Great. Talk about dumb. Now she'd blown his cover and he would hate her.

But he was gesturing toward Reverend Bellingham, who had stood and bowed his head. Anastasia gulped and bowed her own while the minister said grace.

Then the groom's older brother, whose name Anastasia had forgotten, said, "Yes. I'm a lawyer in

Springfield. Have you ever been to Springfield?"

Anastasia hadn't; but when she said that she hadn't, he told her a little about Springfield and it wasn't totally boring.

Amazing, how easy it was to make adult conversation. Anastasia hadn't ever tried it before.

Next she turned to her right, where Uncle Tim was sitting. She said, "I understand you drive a Porsche."

"That's right. Have you ever ridden in a Porsche?" She hadn't; but now she had *another* adult conversation, and it wasn't totally boring either, except that she had never understood a single thing about horsepower and never would. What a great discovery, Anastasia thought. All you have to do is say something about the other person, and then *they* talk and you don't need to. She glanced across the table and saw that Sonya was doing the same thing. She was listening attentively and nodding her head as the usher on her left told her about medical school.

The food — shrimp cocktail, followed by lamb — wasn't a problem. She liked all of it.

The forks weren't a problem. There was just the right number, and she was pretty sure she was using the right ones, and no one seemed to be checking to see if she was, anyway.

And wine wasn't a problem. Anastasia had worried about whether she was supposed to drink wine if they served it, and what her parents would say if she did. But the waiter poured wine into the glasses in front of each adult, and ginger ale into the glasses of the junior bridesmaids. He did it so quietly, without making a big deal, that no one even noticed that hers was ginger ale, and Anastasia was relieved.

She had worried that she wouldn't be able to think of anything else to say to Uncle Tim after she mentioned the Porsche. She didn't know anything else about him except that he led a glamorous life, and she didn't think she could say casually, "I understand that you lead a glamorous life."

But when she noticed that he held his hand over the top of his wine glass and shook his head "no" to the waiter, it gave her a topic of conversation.

"Are you a recovering alcoholic?" Anastasia asked politely.

Uncle Tim looked startled. "No," he said, "as a matter of fact I'm not. But to tell you the truth —" He lowered his voice and glanced around to be sure no one else was listening. "I saw the label on the bottle," he whispered, "and it was a terrible wine. So I decided to skip it."

"No kidding?" Anastasia said. "I didn't know you could tell, from the label. I thought you had to taste it, and if it was terrible, you just got stuck swallowing it and maybe throwing up later."

Uncle Tim laughed, and explained a little about wine to Anastasia.

When he finished, she turned again to the lawyer on her left. "Are you enjoying your wine?" she asked.

He made a slight face. "Not really," he said.

"It's not a good year," Anastasia explained. "There

was too much rain in France that year."

He looked intrigued, so she explained to him about grapes needing the right amount of sun. She took another bite of lamb after she had finished the explanation.

This is so fabulous, Anastasia thought. I'm so good at this. Making conversation and everything. Wait till I tell Mom and Dad how well I did.

Suddenly she was startled by a clinking sound. She looked up. The groom's father was tapping his fork against his water glass. Other people started doing the same thing.

Anastasia didn't have any idea what they were doing. But dutifully she tapped her fork against her glass.

Everyone stopped talking, and the groom's father stood up with his wine glass in his hand. "A toast," he announced in a loud voice, "to the bride and groom! Long life and great happiness to them!"

Everyone raised their glasses, so Anastasia held her ginger ale in the air and took a sip when they did.

The dinner plates were taken away, and dessert arrived. Now there were more clinking glasses and more toasts, some of them sentimental, some of them silly.

Finally Jeff stood up and toasted the bride. "To Kirsten!" he said, and everyone clapped while Kirsten beamed at him. "My solemn vow that I will bring her breakfast in bed every weekend!"

Everyone cheered, including Anastasia, who thought

that was the best idea a husband could have. She thought she might mention it to her father, on her mother's behalf.

"And," Jeff went on with a grin, "that I will never ever use my middle name!"

Everyone cheered and clapped, and Jeff sat down.

"What's the fuss about his middle name?" Uncle Tim asked, leaning over to whisper to Anastasia. "Do you know what his middle name is?"

Anastasia nodded, grinning. "Yes," she told him, "but I promised I'd never tell."

"It can't be all *that* bad," Uncle Tim said. "Middle names are no big deal."

Anastasia disagreed. "I don't have one," she told him, "but if I did, I sure hope it would be just the right one. A wrong middle name would be awful."

Uncle Tim looked a little puzzled. "I can't imagine a *wrong* middle name."

"Well," Anastasia said, "you probably just haven't thought about it much. But think for a minute. What if — well, what if, for example, your parents had given you a middle name of Tom? Then your name would be Tim Tom! Wouldn't that be awful?"

He laughed. "I suppose so. Except that Tim's only a nickname. It's not my real name."

"Oh, of course. I forgot. Tim's a nickname for Timothy. Well, Timothy Tom would *still* sound kind of stupid, in my opinion."

Uncle Tim took a sip of his coffee. "You're right. But my name isn't Timothy. I have a really unusual first name. It's a family name."

"What is it?" Anastasia asked politely.

He chuckled. "Septimus," he said. "My name's Septimus Smith."

*

"Shrimp cocktail. Lamb. Ice cream with strawberry sauce. Yes, it was fine. Yes, I stood up straight. Yes, Kirsten gave us our pearl earrings. And I don't want to talk about it anymore," Anastasia said.

"Why not?" her father asked in surprise.

"Did something go wrong?" her mother asked.

"Everything went just fine. I just don't want to talk about it now," Anastasia said. "I'm tired. I'm going up to bed."

"Well, it *is* late," her mother said, looking at her watch. "And you have a big day tomorrow. Let's see. The wedding's at four. You'll need to wash your hair in the morning so that it has plenty of time to dry. What time should I wake you up?"

"I don't care," Anastasia said miserably, standing on the stairs.

"You know, Mom," she added, "you guys don't *have* to go to the wedding. Sam hates that sailor suit. You could just take him to the zoo or something while *I* go to the wedding. Maybe take him to the Science Museum. They're having a dinosaur exhibition."

"No way," her mother said, laughing. "I wouldn't dream of missing that wedding. I want to see you come down the aisle. I might even weep."

You sure *will* weep, Anastasia thought as she

104

trudged glumly up to her room. You're going to weep the instant Septimus Smith recognizes you from that picture and comes charging across the church saying "Swifty!" And you won't know what he's talking about, and you'll say, "Excuse me? Do you mean my daughter? The kids at school call my *daughter* Swifty!" And Septimus Smith will say —

She closed her bedroom door and sat down on her bed with her shoulders slumped. She couldn't even imagine *what* Septimus Smith would say.

Her mother knocked on the door. "Anastasia?" she called. The door opened.

"Here," she said. "I know you're tired, but I forgot to give you this. It's been on Dad's desk all day. With this wedding excitement, we're all getting absent-minded.

"Good night, sweetie," she said. She put something on the bed, kissed the top of Anastasia's head, and left the room.

Anastasia looked down and picked up the envelope. She sighed. It was one more letter from her pen pal, Septimus Smith.

Dear Swifty,

I'm writing this very quickly before I leave for Boston. I know you told me that your social schedule was very busy this coming week. But when I looked again at your address, I realized that you live very close to the relatives I'll be seeing while I'm there.

So I hope you won't mind if I drop by on Sunday afternoon. I'll be tied up all day Saturday with a family wedding. But I'll plan to stop by briefly on Sunday, maybe just for a quick glass of wine.

About two o'clock? I hope that's okay.

My best,
Septimus Smith

11

Anastasia frowned, and attached the back of the little pearl earring so that it would stay in her ear. She hadn't quite mastered earrings yet, the kind for pierced ears. It was very hard to find the teeny hole. But *there* — they were both attached, now.

She looked gloomily into the mirror. There had been a time — was it only two days ago? — when she might have been completely dazzled by the sight of herself with those pearl earrings on and her long hair tied up on top of her head with the narrow satin ribbon.

Now she just stared at herself and saw the face of a doomed person who within hours was going to be exposed as a fraud.

Her mother appeared at the bedroom door in the flowered silk dress that she was wearing to the wedding.

"I can't believe how gorgeous you look, Anastasia," she said.

"Thank you."

"Aren't you thrilled?"

"Yeah, I guess so. Thrilled."

Her mother looked puzzled. "Do you feel all right, Anastasia? You're not sick, are you?"

"No. I'm okay." Anastasia looked at her mother. "You're not going to wear your hair like that, are you?"

Mrs. Krupnik touched her hair. "I was planning to. What's wrong with it?"

"Just that it's sort of old-fashioned. I mean, it's exactly the way you wore it when you graduated from art school."

Mrs. Krupnik laughed. "I know. Your dad says it makes me look young."

"Well, *that's* what's wrong with it, for Pete's sake. It makes you look too young. You're supposed to look like someone thirty-eight years old, not twenty-two!"

"Come on, Anastasia, don't be such a grouch. Tell you what. If you hate my hair this way, I'll change it, just for you, just to cheer you up. How would you like me to wear it?"

"Could you dye it or something? And cut it short?"

"For heaven's sakes, of course I can't, not in half an hour. I'll pin it back. You have a phone call, by the

108

way. That's what I came up to tell you. It's Daphne. She sounds distressed."

Anastasia started down the stairs to the telephone. On her way she called, "And Mom, you should plan to wear dark glasses. It'll be very bright in the church, with Kirsten's white dress and everything!

"What's up, Daph?" she said into the phone.

"We'll be by to pick you up in twenty minutes. But I'm just calling you and Meredith and Sonya to warn you in advance that there's going to be a scene in the church."

"How did you know?" Anastasia asked. She hadn't told *anyone* about Septimus Smith. "Who told you?"

"My mom told me, of course."

"Well, how on earth did *she* know?"

"She doesn't know *yet*. It's when she finds *out* that there's going to be a scene."

"What on earth are you talking about, Daphne?"

"Frances Bidwell. When she stands up to sing, my mom is going to go berserk. I just thought I'd warn you, so you wouldn't be amazed."

Anastasia sighed. "Okay, I'm warned. But I don't really think it'll be a problem, Daphne. There are going to be *other* weird scenes going on, believe me."

"You don't think my dad's going to say Jeff's middle name, do you? My dad isn't going to say 'Neptune,' is he?"

"Believe me, Daphne. It won't matter if he does."

Anastasia said a quick goodbye and hung up. Upstairs she could hear Sam bellowing. "No one can see my tattoo!" he wailed. "It's all covered up by this dumb *sleeve!*"

She sighed, and remembered that it had been only a few short weeks ago that she had been excited about this wedding. Even yesterday afternoon she had still been excited. But now it just seemed like a nightmare. She wondered if the bride and groom might be feeling the same way.

*

Mrs. Bellingham was driving all four junior bridesmaids to the church. Anastasia had never realized before that there were so many details to sort out for a wedding. She had always assumed that everybody simply showed up at a church, or temple, or city hall, or whatever. Then they got married and they all went home.

But even the transportation was a huge problem to be solved. Kirsten, the bride, was arriving at the church with her parents in a huge white limo. Secretly, Anastasia thought that a limo was sort of gross, and she had decided that she herself would never ride in one unless, of course, she became a movie star or something.

If she ever got married (though she was beginning to be fairly certain that she never would), she would simply ride her bike to the ceremony.

In the car, the four girls admired one another self-consciously. They *did* look beautiful: not at all like the blue-jeaned seventh-graders they ordinarily were.

Anastasia noticed, too, that Mrs. Bellingham —

who had thrown away her Revlon products when she became a feminist — must have sifted through the trash and found a discarded lipstick.

"Okay," Daphne's mother said, looking at her watch after she pulled into the church parking lot, "let's see. It's not quite time. We'll sit here in the car until the last minute. When Kirsten and her parents arrive, we'll know it's time to go up to the entrance."

"We can watch the people go in," Sonya said, squirming in her seat so that she could see the front walk where people were entering the Congregational church. "Look! There's my mom and dad!" She waved, but Dr. and Mrs. Isaacson were talking to each other and didn't notice. They went inside.

"Where are the ushers?" Anastasia asked. She looked around apprehensively, vaguely hoping that Septimus Smith might have sprained his ankle and sent a substitute, the way they did in football games.

"They're already in the church," Mrs. Bellingham explained. "They're helping people to their seats."

Anastasia saw her own family's battered car pull into the parking lot. Her father got out, opened the back door, and lifted Sam from his car seat. One pocket of Sam's sailor suit was bulging, and Anastasia wondered briefly whether he had brought some of his matchbox cars; Sam was so dense about good manners. Mrs. Krupnik got out of the other side of the front seat.

"My mom's not wearing dark glasses!" Anastasia wailed.

Mrs. Bellingham looked puzzled. "Why would she

111

wear dark glasses? Is she having eye problems?"

Anastasia didn't answer. She had thought that maybe — just *maybe* — if her mother changed her hair style and wore dark glasses, Septimus Smith wouldn't recognize her as the person in the picture Anastasia had mailed to him. But now, watching as her parents walked to the church entrance, each holding Sam by a hand, she could see that her mother looked very much as she had the day she graduated from art school seventeen years earlier.

"Shhhh," she whispered. She waited, cringing, for the voice of Septimus Smith shouting "Swifty!" from the interior of the church. She waited for the wedding to be ruined before it began.

But the only sound that drifted through the church entrance was the sound of organ music playing softly.

"Look!" Meredith squealed. "It's *them!*"

Anastasia turned and looked for the limo arriving. But it wasn't the limo. It was Steve Harvey's father, stopping briefly. Steve, Norman, Kirby, and Eddie all climbed out of the car and Mr. Harvey drove away.

"Those *dudes*," Daphne said. All four girls giggled as they watched the boys in their creased slacks, turtlenecks (Norman in a bow tie), and sport coats climb the stairs to the church door and disappear inside.

"They were almost late," Mrs. Bellingham commented. "Here we go, girls. Here comes the limo!"

They got out of the car and shook their dresses free of wrinkles. Holding their long skirts away from the ground carefully, they went to join the bride and her parents at the entrance to the church.

"Mom," Daphne said suddenly. "One thing."

"What's that?" Mrs. Bellingham asked. She was about to go inside to take her seat.

"Whatever happens — I mean, *whatever* happens — don't make a scene, okay?"

Mrs. Bellingham laughed. "I don't make scenes, Daphne. You know that."

"Mrs. Bellingham," Anastasia said, a little embarrassed, "if you sit near my mom, would you tell her the same thing? No scenes?"

Caroline Bellingham shook her head, chuckling. She adjusted the ribbon in Daphne's hair and whispered, "Don't be nervous, any of you. You all look fabulous." She took the arm of an usher and went down the aisle of the church to be seated.

Septimus Smith was standing nearby, wearing a tuxedo, looking glamorous. He grinned and winked at Anastasia. "You kids look great," he said softly.

Anastasia smiled politely and thanked him. Someone handed her a bouquet of mixed pink flowers and nudged her into her place. Behind her, vaguely, she was aware of the swirl of white organdy surrounding the bride.

"Almost time," someone whispered. "Ushers? Is everybody seated?"

The ushers all disappeared through a door. The wedding will be okay, Anastasia was thinking. We'll get through the wedding okay because my mom's just one face in a whole sea of faces in the church and he won't notice her.

And as for the reception — well, just before the

reception I'll tell him that I'm sorry I can't introduce him to my parents because unfortunately their religion doesn't permit them to talk to people wearing tuxedoes —

No. That's dumb. I'll say I can't introduce him because my entire family has regrettably been exposed to smallpox and the doctor said —

"Ready?" a voice was asking her.

Anastasia sighed and straightened her shoulders. "Ready," she whispered.

She peered around the people ahead of her and looked down the long, carpeted aisle of the church. In front of the altar, Daphne's father, Reverend Bellingham, wearing long robes, was smiling. Before him, the groom and best man were standing awkwardly, with self-conscious smiles. The ushers, after seating the last people, had hurried around the back way and now they, too, including Septimus Smith, were arranged at the front of the church, waiting for the wedding procession to start.

The organ music swelled into the opening melody of the wedding march. Ahead of her, she saw Sonya, the first in line of the junior bridesmaids, start walking slowly. After a moment someone nudged Daphne, who moved forward next. Anastasia watched carefully until Daphne was a third of the way down the aisle.

She counted, blinked, took a deep breath, and headed down the aisle herself.

As she walked, moving her feet slowly in the gliding rhythm they had rehearsed, she repeated to herself the humiliating words in the letter she had written late the night before. She had not yet mailed it.

Dear Tim:

Septimus is a pretty nice name, actually, and I hope that you marry someone who lets you use it.

Swifty is a stupid name, and I'm sorry I made it up.

I'm sorry I made *everything* up. If I had known that you were Meredith's uncle, I wouldn't have.

I didn't ever lie in my letters. I *am* young and female and tall and single. You already know that, of course.

I just didn't say *how* young. And you never asked.

I do have a sloop, really. But you never asked me how big it is.

And you only asked for a photograph — you didn't say of me. So the one I sent wasn't really a lie.

But the whole thing was really truly dumb on my part. And the dumbest part is that I got to believing it myself a little bit.

I had already given up boys, or at least the pursuit of boys. Now I have given up the pursuit of men as well.

I am very, very sorry, and I hope the lady who lives in California and has a sloop is still available. Maybe she is even a movie star. But please be sure to check it out and make sure she is telling the truth. I don't want you to have two bad experiences in such a short time.

Sincerely,
Anastasia Krupnik

P.S. If I were still using the name Swifty, which I am not, I would sign this letter:

STUPID WEIRD IDIOTIC FEMALE: TOO YOUNG

12

"I'm exhausted," Mrs. Krupnik said. She kicked off her shoes and sank down on the living room couch. "But I don't know *when* I've had as much fun. That was a wonderful wedding! Did you have as much fun as I did?"

Anastasia undid the ribbon at the top of her head and shook her long hair loose. She grinned and sprawled beside her mother. "Yeah," she said. "I had a terrific time."

Her father entered the living room with his necktie loosened and a beer in his hand. "I took off Sam's shoes, but I put him into bed with his clothes on. He was out like a light," he said.

"Don't you think," he added, "that we could retire

the sailor suit? It really does look stupid. I agree with Sam."

Mrs. Krupnik laughed. "Okay," she said. "It's getting too small for him, anyway."

"How about you, Dad?" Anastasia asked. "Did you have fun at the wedding and the reception?"

He nodded. "I'm not sure *fun* is the correct word for it. It was — well, I'd call it somewhat *surreal*. Especially the wedding itself. Could you please explain to me exactly what was going on at the wedding?"

Anastasia started to laugh. "Didn't you *get it*, Dad?"

He shook his head. "I couldn't figure it out. Everything seemed to be proceeding along just like at every other wedding I've ever been to, and all of a sudden everyone started murmuring. Then chuckling. Then laughing. I started laughing, too, because it was sort of contagious, but I never quite figured out what we were laughing at."

Then he added with a groan, "I don't mean the bell. I figured that out right away, and I grabbed it from Sam as quickly as I could. It's amazing that he could stuff a tricycle bell into the pocket of those pants!"

"I'm going to confiscate that bell for a month," Mrs. Krupnik muttered.

"Mom, do you want to explain the laughing or should I?" Anastasia asked. She was taking off her pearl earrings. Her earlobes ached a little.

"You go ahead, sweetie. It started up in the front of the church, where you were standing."

118

"Well, first of all, when we were at the rehearsal, Reverend Bellingham didn't say all the stuff he was actually going to say at the wedding itself. He just said, 'Then at this part, I'll read a psalm and blah blah blah —"

" 'Blah blah blah'?" her father asked. "He said that?"

"Yeah, just to save time at the rehearsal."

"That sounds irreverent to me. A minister saying 'blah blah blah.' "

"Well, he didn't mean it that way. He was just saving time. But then, at the wedding itself —"

It had started perfectly. It was just like a wedding in a movie. The church was decorated with huge bouquets of pink and white flowers, and it was filled with people whose faces turned to watch as Anastasia followed the other junior bridesmaids down the aisle. Most of them glanced at her and then turned to look at the bride, who followed farther on at the end of the procession, holding her father's arm. But Anastasia could see that a few people — her parents, and Sam, and even, to her surprise, Steve Harvey — kept their eyes on her as she walked slowly, carefully, and a little nervously toward the altar.

Finally she reached the place where she was to stand with the other girls. Across, on the other side, she could see the ushers standing attentively. She looked for a moment at handsome Uncle Tim — Septimus Smith — and thought with despair once again how shocked he would be when he recognized her

119

mother, when Anastasia would have to explain, when she would be humiliated in front of all the guests at the reception. She thought again about the letter of apology she had written, and how she would trudge out to the mailbox tonight to send it to New York.

But when Kirsten, her veil a shimmering white halo around her head, took her place beside the groom, Anastasia put the despair out of her mind and resolved to concentrate on the wedding.

Reverend Bellingham beamed at the congregation and said a few words about the joys of marriage. Anastasia listened with interest, since at the rehearsal he had only indicated by "blah blah blah" what he would say.

"It is always such a pleasure to stand here and watch a beautiful bride walk down the aisle," Reverend Bellingham began.

"Wok," murmured Meredith under her breath. Anastasia suppressed a giggle. Beside her, she felt Daphne stiffen and choke back a laugh.

As the minister talked on, Anastasia saw that Kirsten, beneath her veil, was grinning.

Finally Reverend Bellingham moved to the lectern and began to read a psalm. "The Lord is my shepherd," he read. Anastasia composed her face into a serious look.

"Yea, though I walk through the valley of the shadow —" Reverend Bellingham read.

"Wok," the bride and groom both said together.

Reverend Bellingham looked flustered. He

stopped, smiled awkwardly, and then finished the psalm.

There was a moment of silence. The bride and groom, and all four junior bridesmaids, were biting their lips and looking studiously at the floor.

The organist began to play a piece of music that Anastasia recognized from *Carousel*. Daphne nudged Anastasia with an elbow and gestured slightly with her head toward the balcony. Anastasia looked. Frances Bidwell, wearing a large green hat, had stood and was preparing to sing.

"When you walk through a storm," she sang in her high, loud voice.

"Wok," Anastasia heard herself say aloud. But she wasn't the only one. Daphne, Meredith, Sonya, Kirsten, and Jeff had all said it, too. The congregation chuckled.

The song continued. Anastasia looked out into the church until she found the place where Daphne's mother was sitting. She knew that Daphne thought her mother was going to freak out at this moment, the moment when Frances Bidwell sang. But Daphne's mother had her hand over her mouth, and her shoulders were shaking. She was laughing.

"Walk on, walk on, with hooooppe in your hearrrt," Frances Bidwell sang.

"*Wok*." This time Reverend Bellingham said it, almost like a hiccup. The congregation laughed aloud.

Finally Frances Bidwell came to the dramatic conclusion of the song. She took a deep breath as the organ worked its way with flourishes to the final line.

"You'll neeeever walk aloooone," she sang.

"WOK," sang the bride, the groom, and maid of honor, the best man, the four junior bridesmaids, and all four ushers in unison.

A swell of laughter swept over the church.

Reverend Bellingham, chuckling, moved to his place in front of Kirsten and Jeff, read the vows, waited while the bride and groom each said "I will," and directed the exchange of rings.

"I now pronounce you man and wife," he announced. "May you wok happily together down the pathways of married life!"

The congregation burst into applause and the entire wedding party followed the newly married couple down the aisle. As Anastasia, holding the arm of Septimus Smith, passed the place where her family was sitting, she saw Sam raise his hand, with its tricycle bell, and give a loud *BRRRING* of celebration.

"That's *terrible!*" Myron Krupnik said, after Anastasia had explained the laughter during the ceremony.

Mrs. Krupnik shrugged. "What's so terrible?" she asked. "A wedding is supposed to be a joyous occasion. And the minister didn't seem to mind. Most weddings are so serious and solemn — maybe he liked the change."

"Maybe," her husband acknowledged. "He seemed in good spirits at the reception. I even saw him dancing with his ex-wife."

"Speaking of *dancing*," Anastasia said, remembering something suddenly. "You know what? Me and Meredith and Sonya and Daphne —"

Her father raised his eyebrows at her.

"I meant," she corrected, "Meredith and Sonya and Daphne and I. We invited Steve and Eddie and Norman and Kirby so we'd have somebody to dance with at the reception! And they didn't dance! Not one of them! Not once!"

"Seventh-grade boys *never* dance," her mother pointed out. "You've complained about that to me a million times."

"I know," Anastasia said, making a face. "But we thought they would at a wedding, for Pete's sake! I'm giving up boys for *real*."

"Anyway," Mrs. Krupnik said, "you did dance a lot, Anastasia. Dad danced with you, and —"

Myron Krupnik cringed. "I'm a terrible dancer," he said apologetically. "I hope I didn't ruin those beautiful blue shoes, Anastasia."

Anastasia looked down at the floor, where her shoes were lying by the couch. "They're a little smudged is all," she said. "No problem."

"And you danced with every single usher," her mother went on. "They were really awfully sweet, to dance with you kids."

"Yeah," Anastasia agreed. It was true — each of the ushers had danced with the junior bridesmaids. And her father had danced with her, though he was correct that he was a terrible dancer. Sonya's father, Dr. Isaacson, had danced with her, too.

Steve, Eddie, Kirby, and Norman had spent the entire reception eating endless amounts of food from the buffet table and hanging out near the band, talking to the musicians when they weren't playing. Talk about adolescent behavior.

"About the ushers," her mother was saying.

"What about them?"

"Well, there was one who was especially tall and good-looking. The one who came down the aisle with you, Anastasia, at the end of the ceremony?"

Oh, no, Anastasia thought. I tried so hard to keep them apart. But now is when she's going to say that he came up to her and said, "Hi, Swifty!" and she said, "You must mean my daughter," and then *he* said —

She gulped. "That was, ah, Meredith's Uncle Tim," she said. "Mom," she went on in a nervous voice, "I have a confession to make —"

But her mother wasn't paying attention. "He acted very strange," she said. "He kept staring at me."

"Staring at you?" asked her husband.

"Yes. He stared at me *knowingly*. That's the best way I can describe it. And he kept starting toward me as if he were going to say something."

"Did he? Say anything, I mean?" Anastasia asked apprehensively.

"Good heavens, no. Every time I saw him start toward me with that strange look, I went to the ladies' room. Or I grabbed you, Myron, and started dancing.

"And then, just as we were leaving," her mother

124

added, "he was there in the doorway, and I could *swear* that he whispered, 'See you tomorrow,' when I walked past. Isn't that strange?"

Anastasia felt uneasy. "I understand he's a rather strange person," she said, feeling a little disloyal to Septimus Smith. "He drives a Porsche and leads a glamorous life. I think you were very wise not to talk to him."

"So do I," said her father.

They were all silent for a moment, remembering the wedding. Anastasia was suddenly remembering something else, as well: Septimus Smith would be knocking on the door of her house tomorrow at 2 P.M.

"Mom? Dad?" she asked. "Can we do something tomorrow, just as a family? Can we first go out to brunch, maybe about eleven o'clock, and then after that we can take Sam to the dinosaur exhibition at the Science Museum?"

"Sounds good to me," her father said.

"Sounds *great* to me. I'd love it," her mother said. "I think I'll make a pot of coffee," she added, yawning. "Anastasia, can I get you anything? Milk? A Pepsi?"

"No, thank you. I just remembered something I want to do upstairs."

In her stocking feet, Anastasia went upstairs and into her brother's bedroom, where Sam slept soundly, wearing his sailor suit.

"Sam," she said into his ear, but he didn't stir.

"*Sam*," she said more loudly, and shook his shoulder.

"Mmmmmmm?" Sam murmured.

"I've decided to sell you back your sloop," Anastasia said.

"Mmmmmmm?" He rubbed his eyes sleepily.

"Your *sloop*, Sam. You can buy it back, like you wanted."

"No. I don't wanna." He turned over and buried his face in the pillow."

"But Sam!" She shook him again. "You said you'd give me fifty cents. Remember?"

"No," he said in a muffled voice. "I changed my mind."

"Sam, I really want you to have that sloop back."

He lifted his head, opened his eyes, and looked at her groggily. "You pay *me*, then. A dollar."

"A *dollar?*"

But Sam had put his head back down and was breathing deeply.

Anastasia stared at him for a moment. Finally she sighed. She went to her room, picked up the little red sloop from the windowsill, took a crumpled dollar bill from her wallet, and returned to Sam's bedroom.

"Sam," she said in an irritated voice to her soundly sleeping brother, "you're going to be a great businessman someday. But I hope you have a whole lot of trouble managing your portfolio." She left the sloop and the money on the table beside Sam's bed.

Back in her room, she tore up the letter she had written the night before. She took out a fresh sheet of stationery and began to write a new one.

When her mother knocked on her bedroom door,

Anastasia quickly slid a magazine over the letter.

Mrs. Krupnik entered the room and sat down on Anastasia's bed. "You know," she said, "being at the wedding made me think about what we were talking about recently. All the things you renounce if you renounce marriage."

Anastasia looked at her mother questioningly.

"Did you know that I had a Newfoundland dog when I was a kid?" her mother asked.

"Sure. I've seen a million pictures of you with him. You told me his name was Shadow."

"Right," her mother said, smiling. "Good old Shadow. I really love dogs. But you know your dad's allergic to them. So I've had to —"

"Renounce dogs?"

"Yeah," her mother said sadly. "And also, Anastasia, remember when you asked me what a sloop was? And without even looking it up I was able to tell you what a sloop was? A single-masted sailboat rigged fore and aft?"

"I sold the sloop back to Sam," Anastasia told her.

Her mother chuckled. "Good. He'll be pleased. But listen, Anastasia — the reason I *know* about sloops is because I used to sail a lot when I was young. My father had a sailboat. And I *love* sailing. But when I got married: well, you know that your dad —"

Anastasia nodded. "Seasick," she said. "Dad gets seasick."

Mrs. Krupnik nodded. "I had to renounce sailing," she said with a sigh.

Then she brightened. "But what I wanted to tell

you, Anastasia, is that I don't regret it for one instant. Because look at everything I got in return. Downstairs, in the living room, your dad — he's sound asleep on the couch, with the newspaper over his face, same as always."

Anastasia giggled. "Is he snoring? Is he fluttering the newspaper?"

"Yep." Her mother grinned. "And on the second floor, there's old Sam, sound asleep in his dumb sailor suit, with a three-color tattoo on his arm."

"Good old Sam," Anastasia said, smiling.

"And here, on the third floor, in this messy room —" Her mother looked around Anastasia's bedroom, smiling. She stood up, put her arms around Anastasia, and kissed the top of her head. "I have my wonderful daughter who looked so beautiful today that I almost burst into tears, I was so proud."

"Thanks, Mom," Anastasia said.

"I wouldn't trade any of that for a dog or a sloop," her mother said firmly. She turned to leave. "Oh," she reminded Anastasia from the doorway, "earlier, you started to say that you had a confession to make."

"It was just something dumb," Anastasia said, embarrassed. Quickly, in her mind, she realized that she didn't want to tell her mother about her relationship with Septimus Smith. Now that it was over — and it would be as soon as she mailed this letter in the morning — there was no need for her mother ever to know that she had done something so foolish.

Of course, she realized at the same time, there

128

were plenty of *other* dumb things she could confess.

Her mother waited.

Anastasia shrugged. "Well," she confessed, "it was this. I don't have the slightest idea — not the *slightest* — what a wok is."

Dear Septimus:

I'm sorry that when you came to my house I wasn't at home.

But I must tell you that circumstances have made it necessary to end our correspondence.

After-effects of a recent lobotomy made me realize that I am not ready for a relationship with a man of your sophistication.

If I had a label, like a bottle of wine, you could read it and see that I am the *wrong year* for you.

Also, I have just sold my sloop.

Regretfully yours,
SWIFTY

(Someday — When I'm Fourteen . . . ? Thank You)